Praise for Michael Chabon's *A Model World*

"A delight."
—*People*

"Vignettes of life in the fast and facile lane, limned
in a crisp, bright prose style shot through with
quick-witted insights."
—*Wall Street Journal*

"Michael Chabon gives us characters that are like scattered
socks in a drawer, unpaired or mismatched, isolated,
incomplete. . . . Chabon rises above the gloom and
desperation of these lost worlds with the sheer vitality of
his writing. . . . He writes as if he is expertly flying a kite,
pulling tautly on the strings, then letting loose in
swirling narrative flights."
—*Philadelphia Inquirer*

"Wonderfully wry . . . a lively, intelligent writer. . . . Chabon
takes on the terrible twenties with a fine eye
and an eloquent tongue."
—*Boston Globe*

"Chabon manages to locate those fleeting moments that
define a young man's initiation into the complexities of
the grown-up world, and to memorialize those moments
with such precision that they glow with the hard, radiant
energy of one's own remembered past."
—*New York Times*

About the Author

MICHAEL CHABON is the Pulitzer Prize–winning author of *The Amazing Adventures of Kavalier & Clay*, *Wonder Boys*, *The Mysteries of Pittsburgh*, *Werewolves in Their Youth*, *Summerland*, and *The Final Solution*. He lives in Berkeley, California, with his wife, novelist Ayelet Waldman, and their children.

A Model World
And Other Stories

Michael Chabon

HARPER **PERENNIAL**

HARPER ● PERENNIAL

The stories in this collection were originally published in the following: *Gentleman's Quarterly*: "More than Human" (1989); *Mademoiselle*: "Blumenthal on the Air" (1987); *The New Yorker*: "Admirals" (1987), "The Halloween Party" (1988), "The Little Knife" (1988), "The Lost World" (1990), "Millionaires" (1990), "A Model World" (1989), "Ocean Avenue" (1989), "S ANGEL" (1990), and "Smoke" (1990).

A hardcover edition of this book was published in 1992 by Avon Books.

HarperCollins books may be purchased for educational, business, or sales promotional use. For information please write: Special Markets Department, HarperCollins Publishers, 10 East 53rd Street, New York, NY 10022.

First Avon edition published 1992.
First Bard edition published 1998.
First Perennial edition published 2000.
Reissued in Harper Perennial 2005.

Library of Congress Cataloging-in-Publication Data is available upon request.
ISBN-10: 0-06-079060-1
ISBN-13: 978-0-06-079060-8

07 08 09 ❖/RRD 10 9 8 7 6 5 4

To the memory of Ernest Cohen

The author is very grateful to Mr. Daniel Menaker, to Mr. Douglas Stumpf, to Ms. Mary Evans, and to Ms. Lollie Groth.

CONTENTS

———————

More delicate than the historians' are the map makers' colors.

—ELIZABETH BISHOP

PART I

A MODEL WORLD

S ANGEL

On the morning of his cousin's wedding Ira performed his toilet, as he always did, with patience, hope, and a ruthless punctilio. He put on his Italian wool trousers, his silk shirt, his pink socks, to which he imputed a certain sexual felicity, and a slightly worn but still serviceable Willi Smith sport jacket. He shaved the delta of skin between his eyebrows and took a few extra minutes to clean out the inside of his car, a battered, faintly malodorous Japanese hatchback of no character whatever. Ira never went anywhere without expecting that when he arrived there he would meet the woman with whom he had been destined to fall in love. He drove across Los Angeles from Palms to Arcadia, where his cousin Sheila was being married in a synagogue Ira got lost trying to find. When he walked in late he disturbed the people sitting at the back of the shul, and his aunt Lillian, when he joined her, pinched his arm quite painfully. The congregation was dour and Conservative, and as the ceremony dragged on Ira found himself awash in a nostalgic tedium, and he fell to wishing for irretrievable things.

At the reception that followed, in the banquet room of

the old El Imperio Hotel in Pasadena, he looked in vain for one of his more interesting young female cousins, such as Zipporah from Berkeley, who was six feet tall and on the women's crew at Cal, or that scary one, Leah Black, who had twice, in their childhoods, allowed Ira to see what he wanted to see. Both Ira and Sheila sprang from a rather disreputable branch of Wisemans, however, and her wedding was poorly attended by the family. All the people at Ira's table were of the groom's party, except for Ira's greataunts, Lillian and Sophie, and Sophie's second husband, Mr. Lapidus.

"You need a new sport jacket," said Aunt Sophie.

"He needs a new *watch*," said Aunt Lillian.

Mr. Lapidus said that what Ira needed was a new barber. A lively discussion arose at table 17, as the older people began to complain about contemporary hairstyles, with Ira's itself—there was some fancy clipperwork involved—cited frequently as an instance of their inscrutability. Ira zoned out and ate three or four pounds of the salmon carpaccio with lemon cucumber and cilantro that the waiters kept bringing around, and also a substantial number of boletus-mushroom-and-goat-cheese profiteroles. He watched the orchestra members, particularly the suave-looking black tenor saxophonist with dreadlocks, and tried to imagine what they were thinking about as they blew all that corny cha-cha-cha. He watched Sheila and her new husband whispering and box-stepping, and undertook the same experiment. She seemed pleased enough—smiling and flushed and mad to be wearing that dazzling dress—but she didn't look like she was in love, as he imagined love to look. Her eye was restive, vaguely troubled, as though she were trying to remember exactly who this man was with his arms around her waist, tipping her backward on one leg and planting a kiss on her throat.

It was as he watched Sheila and Barry walk off the dance floor that the woman in the blue dress caught Ira's eye, then looked away. She was sitting with two other women, at a table under one of the giant palm trees that stood in pots all across the banquet room, which the hotel called the Oasis Room and had been decorated to suit. When Ira returned her gaze he felt a pleasant internal flush, as though he had just knocked back a shot of whiskey. The woman's expression verged a moment on nearsightedness before collapsing into a vaguely irritable scowl. Her hair was frizzy and tinted blond, her lips were thick and red but grim and disapproving, and her eyes, which might have been gray or brown, were painted to match her electric dress. Subsequent checking revealed that her body had aged better than her fading face, which nonetheless he found beautiful, and in which, in the skin at her throat and around her eyes, he thought he read strife and sad experience and a willingness to try her luck.

Ira stood and approached the woman, on the pretext of going over to the bar, a course which required that he pass her table. As he did so he stole another long look, and eavesdropped on an instant of her conversation. Her voice was soft and just a little woeful as she addressed the women beside her, saying something deprecating, it seemed to Ira, about lawyers' shoes. The holes in her earlobes were filled with simple gold posts. Ira swung like a comet past the table, trailing, as he supposed, a sparkling wake of lustfulness and Eau Sauvage, but she seemed not to notice him, and when he reached the bar he found, to his surprise, that he genuinely wanted a drink. His body was unpredictable and resourceful in malfunction, and he was not, as a result, much of a drinker; but it was an open bar, after all. He ordered a double shot of Sauza.

There were two men talking behind him, waiting for their drinks, and Ira edged a little closer to them, without turning around, so that he could hear better. He was a fourth-year drama student at UCLA and diligent about such valuable actorly exercises as eavesdropping, spying, and telling complicated lies to fellow passengers on airplanes.

"That Charlotte was a class A, top-of-the-line, capital B-I-T bitch," said one of the men, in the silky tones of an announcer on a classical music station. "And fucked up from her ass to her eyebrows." He had a very faint New York accent.

"Exactly, exactly," said the other, who sounded older, and well-accustomed to handing out obsequious counsel to young men. "No question. You had to fire her."

"I should have done it the day it happened. Ha ha. Pow, fired in her own bed."

"Exactly. Ha ha."

"Ira!" It was his cousin, the bride, bright and still pink from dancing. Sheila had long, kinky black hair, spectacular eyelashes, and a nose that, like Ira's, flirted dangerously, but on the whole successfully, with immenseness. He thought she looked really terrific, and he congratulated her wistfully. Ira and Sheila had at one time been close. Sheila hung an arm around his neck and kissed him on the cheek. Her breath blew warm in his ear. "What is that you're drinking?"

"Tequila," he said. He turned to try to get a glimpse of the men at the bar, but it was too late. They had been replaced by a couple of elderly women with empty highball glasses and giant clip-on earrings.

"Can I try?" She sipped at it and made a face. "I hope it makes you feel better than it tastes."

"It couldn't," Ira said, taking a more appreciative pull of his own.

Sheila studied his face, biting at her lip. They hadn't seen one another since the evening, over a year before, when she had taken him to see some dull and infuriating Soviet movie—*Shadow of Uzbek Love,* or something like that—at UCLA. She was looking, it seemed to him, for signs of change.

"So are you dating anyone?" she said, and there was a glint of tension in her casual tone.

"Lots of people."

"Uh huh. Do you want to meet someone?"

"No thanks." Things had gotten a little wiggly, Ira now recalled, in the car on the way home from Westwood that night. Sheila drove one of those tiny Italian two-seaters capable of filling very rapidly with sexual tension, in particular at a stop light, with Marvin Gaye coming over the radio and a pretty cousin in the driver's seat, chewing thoughtfully on a strand of hair. Ira, in a sort of art-house funk, had soon found himself babbling on about Marx and George Orwell and McCarthyism, and praying for green lights; and when they arrived at his place he had dashed up the steps into his apartment and locked the door behind him. He shook his head, wondering at this demureness, and drained the glass of tequila. He said, "Do you want to dance?"

They went out onto the floor and spun around a few times slowly to "I'll Never Be the Same." Sheila felt at once soft and starchy in her taffeta dress, gigantic and light as down.

"I really wish you would meet my friend Carmen," said Sheila. "She needs to meet a nice man. She lives next door to my parents in Altadena. Her husband used to beat her but now they're divorced. She has the most beautiful gray eyes."

At this Ira stiffened, and he blew the count.

"Sitting right over there under the palm tree? In the blue dress?"

"Ouch! That's my foot."

"Sorry."

"So you noticed her! Great. Go on, I., ask her to dance. She's so lonesome anymore."

The information that the older woman might actually welcome his overtures put him off, and somehow made him less certain of success. Ira tried to formulate a plausible excuse.

"She looks mean," he said. "She gave me a nasty look not five minutes ago. Oh, hey. It's Donna."

"Donna!"

Donna Furman, in a sharp gray sharkskin suit, approached and kissed the bride, first on the hand with the ring, then once on each cheek, in a gesture that struck Ira as oddly papal and totally Hollywood. Donna started to tell Sheila how beautiful she looked, but then some people with cameras came by and swept Sheila away, so Donna threw out her arms to Ira, and the cousins embraced. She wore her short hair slicked back with something that had an ozone smell and it crackled against Ira's ear. Donna was a very distant relation, and several years older than Ira, but as the Furmans had lived in Glassell Park, not far from Ira's family in Mt. Washington, Ira had known Donna all his life, and he was glad to see her.

This feeling of gladness was not entirely justified by recent history, as Donna, a girl with a clever tongue and a scheming imagination, had grown into a charming but unreliable woman, and if Ira had stopped to consider he might, at first, have had a bone or two to pick with his fourth cousin once removed. She was a good-looking, dark-complected lesbian—way out in the open about that—with a big bust and a twelve-thousand-dollar smile. The vein of roguery that had found its purest expression in Sheila's grandfather, Milton Wiseman, a manufacturer of diet powders and placebo aphrodisiacs, ran thin but rich through Donna's character. She talked fast and took recondite drugs and told funny stories about famous people whom she claimed to know. Despite the fact that she worked for one of the big talent agencies in Culver City, in their music division, and made ten times what Ira did waiting tables and working summers at a Jewish drama camp up in Idyllwild, Donna nonetheless owed Ira, at the time of this fond embrace, three hundred and twenty-five dollars.

"We ought to go out to Santa Anita tonight," Donna said, winking one of her moist brown eyes, which she had inherited from her mother, a concentration camp survivor, a Hollywood costume designer, and a very sweet lady who had taken an overdose of sleeping pills when Donna was still a teenager. Donna's round, sorrowful eyes made it impossible to doubt that somewhere deep within her lay a wise and tormented soul; in her line of work they were her trump card.

"I'd love to," said Ira. "You can stake me three hundred and twenty-five bucks."

"Oh, right! I forgot about that!" Donna said, squeezing Ira's hand. "I have my checkbook in the car."

"I heard you brought a date, Donna," Ira went on, not wanting to bring out the squirreliness in his cousin right off the bat. When Donna began to squeeze your hand it was generally a portent of fictions and false rationales. She was big on touching, which was all right with Ira. He liked being touched. "So where is the unfortunate girl?"

"Over there," Donna said, inclining her head toward Ira as though what she was about to say were inside information capable of toppling a regime or piling up a fortune in a single afternoon. "At that table under the palm tree, there. With those other two women. The tall one in the flowery thing, with the pointy nose. Her name's Audrey."

"Does she work with you?" said Ira, happy to have an excuse to stare openly at Carmen, seated to the right of Donna's date and now looking back at Ira in a way that, he thought, could hardly be mistaken. He wiggled his toes a few times within his lucky pink socks. Donna's date,

Audrey, waved her fingers at them. She was pretty, with an expensive, blunt hairdo and blue eyes, although her nose was as pointed as a marionette's.

"She lives in my building. Audrey's at the top, at the very summit, I., of a *vast* vitamin pyramid. Like, we're talking, I don't know, ten thousand people, from Oxnard to Norco. Here, I'll take you over." She took hold of the sleeve of Ira's jacket, then noticed the empty shot glass in his hand. "Hold on, let me buy you a drink." This was said without a trace of irony. "Drinking shots?"

"Sauza. Two story."

"A C.C. and water with a twist and a double Sauza," she said to the bartender. "Tequila makes you unlucky with women."

"See that blonde Audrey is sitting beside?"

"Yeah? With the nasty mouth?"

"I'd like to be unlucky with her."

"Drink this," said Donna, handing Ira a shot glass filled to the brim with liquid the very hue of hangover and remorse. "From what I heard she's a basket case, I. Bad husband. A big mess. She keeps taking these beta-carotene tablets every time she has a Seven and Seven, like it's some kind of post-divorce diet or I don't know."

"I think she likes me." They had started toward the table but stopped now to convene a hasty parley on the dance floor, beneath the frond of a squat fan palm. Donna had been giving Ira sexual advice since he was nine.

"How old are you now, twenty-one?"

"Almost."

"She's older than I am, Ira!" Donna patted herself on

the chest. "You don't want to get involved with someone so old. You want someone who still has all her delusions intact, or whatever."

Ira studied Carmen as his cousin spoke, sensing the truth in what she said. He had yet to fall in love to the degree that he felt he was capable of falling, had never written villanelles or declarations veiled in careful metaphor, nor sold his blood plasma to buy champagne or jonquils, nor haunted a mailbox or a phone booth or a certain café, nor screamed his beloved's name in the streets at three in the morning, heedless of the neighbors, and it seemed possible that to fall for a woman who had been around the block a few times might be to rob himself of much of the purely ornamental elements, the swags and antimacassars of first love. No doubt Carmen had had enough of such things. And yet it was her look of disillusion, of detachment, those stoical blue eyes in the middle of that lovely, beaten face, that most attracted him. It would be wrong to love her, he could see that; but he believed that every great love was in some measure a terrible mistake.

"Just introduce me to her, Donnie," he said, "and you don't have to pay me back."

"Pay you back what?" said Donna, lighting up her halogen smile.

She *was* a basket case. The terra cotta ashtray before her on the table, stamped with the words EL IMPERIO, was choked with the slender butts of her cigarettes, and the lit square she held in her long, pretty fingers was trembling noticeably and spewing a huge, nervous chaos of smoke.

Her gray eyes were large and moist and pink as though she had been crying not five minutes ago, and when Donna, introducing Ira, laid a hand on her shoulder, it looked as though Carmen might start in again, from the shock and the unexpected softness of this touch. All of these might have escaped Ira's notice or been otherwise explained, but on the empty seat beside her, where Ira hoped to install himself, sat her handbag, unfastened and gaping, and one glimpse of it was enough to convince Ira that Carmen was a woman out of control. Amid a blizzard of wadded florets of Kleenex, enough to decorate a small parade float, Ira spotted a miniature bottle of airline gin, a plastic bag of jellybeans (all black ones), two unidentifiable vials of prescription medication, a crumpled and torn road map, the wreckage of a Hershey bar, and a key chain, in the shape of a brontosaurus, with one sad key on it. The map was bent and misfolded in such a way that only the fragmentary words S ANGEL, in one corner, were legible.

"Carmen Wallace, this is my adorable little cousin Ira," Donna said, using the hand that was not resting on Carmen's bare shoulder to pull at Ira's cheek. "He asked to meet you."

"How do you do," said Ira, blushing badly.

"Hi," Carmen said, setting her cigarette on the indented lip of the ashtray and extending the tips of her fingers toward Ira, who paused a moment—channeling all of his sexual energy into the center of his right palm—then took them. They were soft and gone in an instant, withdrawn as though he had burned her.

"And this is Audrey—"

"Hi, Audrey."

"—and Doreen, who's a—friend?—of the groom's."

Ira shook hands with these two and, once Carmen had moved her appalling purse onto the floor beside her to make room for him, soon found himself in the enviable position of being the only man at a table of five. Doreen was wearing a bright yellow dress with an extremely open bodice; she had come to her friend Barry's wedding exposing such a great deal of her remarkable chest that Ira wondered about her motives. She was otherwise a little on the plain side and she had a sour, horsey laugh, but she was in real estate and Donna and Audrey, who were thinking of buying a house together, seemed to have a lot to say to her. There was nothing for him and Carmen to do but speak to each other.

"Sheila says you live next door to her folks?" Ira said. Carmen nodded, then turned her head to exhale a long jet of smoke. The contact of their eyes was brief but he thought it had something to it. There was about an inch and a half of Sauza left in Ira's glass and he drained a quarter inch of it, figuring this left him with enough to get through another five questions. He could already tell that talking to Carmen was not going to be easy, but he considered this an excellent omen. Easy flirtation had always struck him as an end in itself and one which did not particularly interest him.

"Is it that big wooden house with the sort of, I don't know, those *things*, those rafters or whatever, sticking out from under all the roofs?" He spread the fingers of one hand and slid them under the other until they protruded, making a crude approximation of the overhanging eaves of a California bungalow. There was such a grand old house, to the north of Sheila's parents, that he'd always admired.

Another nod. She had a habit of opening her eyes very wide, every so often, almost a tic, and Ira wondered if her contact lenses might not be slipping.

"It's a Hetrick and Dewitt," she said bitterly, as though this were the most withering pair of epithets that could be applied to a house. These were the first words she had addressed to him and in them, though he didn't know what she was talking about, he sensed a story. He took another little sip of tequila and nodded agreeably.

"You live in a Hetrick and Dewitt?" said Doreen, interrupting her conversation with Donna and Audrey to reach across Audrey's lap and tap Carmen on the arm. She looked amazed. "Which one?"

"It's the big pretentious one on Orange Blossom, in Altadena," Carmen said, stubbing out her cigarette. She gave a very caustic sigh and then rose to her feet; she was taller than Ira had thought. Having risen to her feet rather dramatically, she now seemed uncertain of what to do next and stood wavering a little on her blue spike heels. It was clear she felt that she had been wrong to come to Sheila's wedding, but that was all she seemed able to manage, and after a moment she sank slowly back into her seat. Ira felt very sorry for her and tried to think of something she could do besides sit and look miserable. At that moment the band launched into "Night and Day," and Ira happened to look toward the table where he had left his aunts. Mr. Lapidus was pulling out his aunt Sophie's chair and taking her arm. They were going to dance.

"Carmen, would you like to dance?" Ira said, blushing, and wiggling his toes.

Her reply was no more than a whisper, and Ira wasn't sure if he heard it correctly, but it seemed to him that she said, "Anything."

They walked, separately, out to the dance floor, and turned to face each other. For an awful moment they just stood, tapping their hesitant feet. But the two old people were describing a slow arc in Ira's general direction, and finally in order to forestall any embarrassing exhortations from Mr. Lapidus, who was known for such things, Ira reached out and took Carmen by the waist and palm, and twirled her off across the wide parquet floor of the Oasis Room. It was an old-fashioned sort of tune and there was no question of their dancing to it any way but in each other's arms.

"You're good at this," Carmen said, smiling for the first time that he could remember.

"Thanks," said Ira. He was in fact a competent dancer—his mother, preparing him for a fantastic and outmoded destiny, had taught him a handful of hokey old steps. Carmen danced beautifully, and he saw to his delight that he had somehow hit upon the precise activity to bring her, for the moment anyway, out of her beta-carotene and black jellybean gloom. "So are you."

"I used to work at the Arthur Murray on La Cienega," she said, moving one hand a little lower on his back. "That was fifteen years ago."

This apparently wistful thought seemed to revive her accustomed gloominess a little, and she took on the faraway, hollow expression of a taxi dancer, and grew heavy in his arms. The action of her legs became overly thoughtful and accurate. Ira searched for something to talk about, to distract her with, but all of the questions he came up with had to do, at least in some respect, with *her,* and he sensed that anything on this subject might plunge her, despite her easy two-step, into an irrevocable sadness. At last the bubble of silence between them grew too great, and Ira pierced it helplessly.

"Where did you grow up?" he said, looking away as he spoke.

"In hotels," said Carmen, and that was that. "I don't think Sheila is happy, do you?" She coughed, and then the song came abruptly to an end. The bandleader set down his trumpet, tugged the microphone up to his mouth, and announced that in just a few short moments the cake was going to be cut.

When they returned to the table a tall, handsome man, his black hair thinning but his chin cleft and his eyes pale green, was standing behind Carmen's empty chair, leaning against it and talking to Donna, Audrey, and Doreen. He wore a fancy, European-cut worsted suit, a purple and sky blue paisley necktie, a blazing white-on-white shirt, and a tiny sparkler in the lobe of his left ear. His nose was large, bigger even than Ira's, and of a complex shape, like the blade of some highly specialized tool; it dominated his face in a way that made the man himself seem dominating. The shining fabric of his suit jacket caught and stretched across the muscles of his shoulders. When Carmen approached her place at the table, he drew her chair for her. She thanked him with a happy and astonishingly carnal smile, and as she sat down he peered, with a polished audacity that made Ira wince in envy, into the scooped neck of her dress.

"Carmen, Ira," said Doreen, "this is Jeff Freebone." As Doreen introduced the handsome Mr. Freebone, all of the skin that was visible across her body colored a rich blood-orange red. Ira's hand vanished momentarily into a tanned, forehand-smashing grip. Ira looked at Donna, hoping to see at least some hint of unimpressedness in her lesbian and often cynical gaze, but his cousin had the same shining-eyed sort of *Tiger Beat* expression on her face as Doreen and Carmen—and Audrey, for that matter—and Ira realized that Jeff Freebone must be very, very rich.

"What's up, Ira?" he said, in a smooth, flattened-out baritone to which there clung a faint tang of New York City, and Ira recognized him, with a start, as the coarse man at the bar who had fired an unfortunate woman named Charlotte in her own bed.

"Jeff here used to work in the same office as Barry and me," Doreen told Carmen. "Now he has his own company."

"Freebone Properties," Carmen said, looking more animated than she had all afternoon. "I've seen the signs on front lawns, right?"

"Billboards," said Donna. "Ads on TV."

"How was the wedding?" Jeff wanted to know. He went around Carmen and sat down in the chair beside her, leaving Ira to stand, off to one side, glowering at his cousin Donna, who was clearly going to leave him high and dry in this. "Did they stand under that tent thing and break the mirror or whatever?"

Ira was momentarily surprised, and gratified, by this display of ignorance, since he had taken Jeff for Jewish. Then he remembered that many of Donna's Hollywood friends spoke with a shmoozing accent whether they were Jewish or not, even ex-cheerleaders from Ames, Iowa, and men named Lars.

"It was weird," Carmen declared, without elaborating—not even Jeff Freebone, apparently, could draw her out—and the degree of acquiescence this judgment received at the table shocked Ira. He turned to seek out Sheila among the hundreds of faces that filled the Oasis Room, to see if she was all right, but could not find her. There was a small crowd gathered around the cathedral cake at the far end of the room, but the bride did not seem to be among them. Weird—what had been weird about it? Was Sheila not, after all, in love with her two hours' husband? Ira tapped his foot to the music, self-conscious, and pretended to continue his search for Sheila, although in truth he was not looking at anything anymore. He was mortified by the quickness with which his love affair with the sad and beautiful woman of his dreams had been derailed, and all at once—the tequila he had drunk had begun to betray him—he came face to face with the distinct possibility that not only would he never find the one he was meant to find, but that no else ever did, either. The discussion around the table hurtled off into the imaginary and vertiginous world of real estate. Finally he had to take hold of a nearby chair and sit down.

"I can get you three mil for it, sight unseen," Jeff Free-bone was declaring. He leaned back in his seat and folded his hands behind his head.

"It's worth way more," said Donna, giving Carmen a poke in the ribs. "It's a work of art, Jeff."

"It's a Hetrick and Dewitt," said everyone at the table, all at once.

"You have to see it," Doreen said.

"All right then, let's see it. I drove my Rover, we can all fit. Take me to see it."

There was moment of hesitation, during which the four women seemed to consider the dictates of decorum and the possible implications of the proposed expedition to see the house that Carmen hated.

"The cake is always like sliced cardboard at these things, anyway," said Donna.

This seemed to decide them, and there followed a general scraping of chairs and gathering of summer wraps.

"Aren't you coming?" said Donna, leaning over Ira—who had settled into a miserable, comfortable slouch—and whispering into his ear. The others were already making their way out of the Oasis Room. Ira scowled at her.

"Hey, come on, I. She needs a realtor, not a lover. Besides, she was way too old for you." She put her arms around his neck and kissed the top of his head. "Okay, sulk. I'll call you." Then she buttoned her sharkskin jacket and turned on one heel.

After Ira had been sitting alone at the table for several minutes, half hoping his aunt Lillian would notice his distress and bring over a piece of cake or a petit four and a plateful of her comforting platitudes, he noticed that Carmen, not too surprisingly, had left her handbag behind. He got up from his chair and went to pick it up. For a moment he peered into it, aroused, despite himself, by the intimacy of this act, like reading a woman's diary, or putting one's hand inside her empty shoe. Then he remembered his disappointment and his anger, and his fist closed around one of the vials of pills, which he quickly slipped into his pocket.

"Ira, have you seen Sheila?"

Ira dropped the purse, and whirled around. It was indeed his aunt Lillian but she looked very distracted and didn't seem aware of having caught Ira in the act. She kept tugging at the fringes of her wildly patterned scarf.

"Not recently," said Ira. "Why?"

Aunt Lillian explained that someone, having drunk too much, had fallen onto the train of Sheila's gown and torn it slightly; this had seemed to upset Sheila a good deal and she had gone off somewhere, no one knew where. The bathrooms and the lobbies of the hotel had all been checked. The cake-cutting was fifteen minutes overdue.

"I'll find her," said Ira.

He went out into the high, cool lobby and crossed it several times, his heels clattering across the marble floors and his soles susurrant along the Persian carpets. He climbed a massive oak staircase to the mezzanine, where he passed through a pair of French doors that opened onto a long balcony overlooking the sparkling pool. Here he found her, dropped in one corner of the terrace like a blown flower. She had taken the garland from her brow and was twirling it around and around in front of her face with the mopey fascination of a child. When she felt Ira's presence she turned, and, seeing him, broke out in a teary-eyed grin that he found very difficult to bear. He walked over to her and sat down beside her on the rough stucco deck of the balcony.

"Hi," he said.

"Are they all going nuts down there?"

"I guess. I heard about your dress. I'm really sorry."

"It's all right." She stared through the posts of the balustrade at the great red sun going down over Santa Monica. There had been a lot of rain the past few days and the air was heartbreakingly clear. "You just feel like such a, I don't know, a big stupid puppet or something, getting pulled around."

Ira edged a little closer to his cousin and she laid her head against his shoulder, and sighed. The contact of her body was so welcome and unsurprising that it frightened him, and he began to fidget with the vial in his pocket.

"What's that?" she said, at the faint rattle.

He withdrew the little bottle and held it up to the dying light. There was no label of any kind on its side.

"I sort of stole them from your friend Carmen."

Sheila managed an offhand smile.

"Oh—how did that work out? I saw you dancing."

"She wasn't for me," said Ira. He unscrewed the cap and tipped the vial into his hand. There were only two pills left, small, pink, shaped like commas—two little pink teardrops. "Any idea what these are? Could they be beta-carotene?"

Sheila shook her head and extended one hand, palm

upward. At first Ira thought she wanted him to place one of the pills upon it, but she shook her head again; when he took her outstretched fingers in his she nodded.

"Ira," she said in the heaviest of voices, bringing her bridal mouth toward his. Just before he kissed her he closed his eyes, brought his own hand to his mouth, and swallowed, hard.

"My darling," he said.

OCEAN
AVENUE

If you can still see how you could once have loved a person, you are still in love; an extinct love is always wholly incredible. One day not too long ago, in Laguna Beach, California, an architect named Bobby Lazar went downtown to have a cup of coffee at the Café Zinc with his friend Albert Wong and Albert's new wife, Dawn (who had, very sensibly, retained her maiden name). Albert and Dawn were still in that period of total astonishment that follows a wedding, grinning at each other like two people who have survived an air crash without a scratch, touching one another frequently, lucky to be alive. Lazar was not a cynical man and he wished them well, but he had also been lonely for a long time, and their happiness was making him a little sick. Albert had brought along a copy of *Science*, in which he had recently published some work on the String Theory, and it was as Lazar looked up from Al's name and abbreviations in the journal's table of contents that he saw Suzette, in her exercise clothes, coming toward the café from across the street, looking like she weighed about seventy-five pounds.

She was always too thin, though at the time of their

closest acquaintance he had thought he liked a woman with bony shoulders. She had a bony back, too, he suddenly remembered, like a marimba, as well as a pointed, bony nose and chin, and she was always—but *always*—on a diet, even though she had a naturally small appetite and danced aerobically or ran five miles every day. Her face looked hollowed and somehow mutated, as do the faces of most women who get too much exercise, but there was a sheen on her brow and a mad, aerobic glimmer in her eye. She'd permed her hair since he last saw her, and it flew out around her head in two square feet of golden Pre-Raphaelite rotini—the lily maid of Astolat on an endorphin high. A friend had once said she was the kind of woman who causes automobile accidents when she walks down the street, and, as a matter of fact, as she stepped up onto the patio of the café, a man passing on his bicycle made the mistake of following her with his eyes for a moment and nearly rode into the open door of a parked car.

"Isn't that Suzette?" Al said. Albert was, as it happened, the only one of his friends after the judgment who refused to behave as though Suzette had never existed, and he was always asking after her in his pointed, physicistic manner, one skeptical eyebrow raised. Needless to say, Lazar did not like to be reminded. In the course of their affair, he knew, he had been terribly erratic, by turns tightfisted and profligate, glum and overeager, unsociable and socially aflutter, full of both flattery and glib invective—a shithead, in short—and, to his credit, he was afraid that he had treated Suzette very badly. It may have been this repressed consciousness, more than anything else, that led him to tell himself, when he first saw her again, that he did not love her anymore.

"Uh-oh," said Dawn, after she remembered who Suzette was.

"I have nothing to be afraid of," Lazar said. As she passed, he called out, "Suzette?" He felt curiously invulnerable to her still evident charms, and uttered her name with the lightness and faint derision of someone on a crowded airplane signaling to an attractive but slightly elderly stewardess. "Hey, Suze!"

She was wearing a Walkman, however, with the earphones turned up very loud, and she floated past on a swell of Chaka Khan and Rufus.

"Didn't she hear you?" said Albert, looking surprised.

"No, Dr. Five Useful Non-Implications of the String Theory, she did not," Lazar said. "She was wearing *earphones*."

"I think she was ignoring you." Albert turned to his bride and duly consulted her. "Didn't she look like she heard him? Didn't her face kind of blink?"

"There she is, Bobby," said Dawn, pointing toward the entrance of the café. As it was a beautiful December morning, they were sitting out on the patio, and Lazar had his back to the Zinc. "Waiting on line."

He felt that he did not actually desire to speak to her but that Albert and Dawn's presence forced him into it somehow. A certain tyranny of in-touchness holds sway in that part of the world—a compulsion to behave always as though one is still in therapy but making real progress, and the rules of enlightened behavior seemed to dictate that he not sneak away from the table with his head under a news-paper—as he might have done if alone—and go home to watch the Weather Channel or Home Shopping Network for three hours with a twelve-pack of Mexican beer and the phone off the hook. He turned around in his chair and looked at Suzette more closely. She had on one of those glittering, opalescent Intergalactic Amazon leotard-and-tights combinations that seem to be made of cavorite or adamantium and do not so much cling to a woman's body as seal her off from gamma rays and lethal stardust. Lazar pronounced her name again, more loudly, calling out across the sunny patio. She looked even thinner from behind.

"Oh, Bobby," she said, removing the headphones but keeping her place in the coffee line.

"Hello, Suze," he said. They nodded pleasantly to one another, and that might have been it right there. After a second or two she dipped her head semiapologetically, smiled an irritated smile, and put the earphones—"ear-buds," he recalled, was the nauseous term—back into her ears.

"She looks great," Lazar said magnanimously to Albert and Dawn, keeping his eyes on Suzette.

"She looks so thin, so drawn," said Dawn, who frankly could have stood to drop about fifteen pounds.

"She looks fine to me," said Al. "I'd say she looks better than ever."

"I know you would," Lazar snapped. "You'd say it just to bug me."

He was a little irritated himself now. The memory of their last few days together had returned to him, despite all his heroic efforts over the past months to repress it utterly. He thought of the weekend following that bad review of their restaurant in the *Times* (they'd had a Balearic restaurant called Ibiza in San Clemente)—a review in which the critic had singled out his distressed-stucco interior and Suzette's Majorcan paella, in particular, for censure. Since these were precisely the two points around which, in the course of opening the restaurant, they had constructed their most idiotic and horrible arguments, the unfavorable notice hit their already shaky relationship like a dumdum bullet, and Suzette went a little nuts. She didn't show up at home or at Ibiza all the next day—so that poor hypersensitive little José had to do all the cooking—but instead disappeared into the haunts of physical culture. She worked out at the gym, went to Zahava's class, had her body waxed, and then, to top it all off, rode her bicycle all the way to El Toro and back. When she finally came home she was in a mighty hormonal rage and suffered under the delusion that she could lift a thousand pounds and chew her way through vanadium steel. She claimed that Lazar had bankrupted her, among other outrageous and untrue assertions, and he went out for a beer to escape from her. By the time he returned, several hours later, she had moved out, taking with her *only his belongings*, as though she had come to see some fundamental inequity in their relationship—such as their having been switched at birth—and were attempting in this way to rectify it.

This loss, though painful, he would have been willing to suffer if it hadn't included his collection of William Powelliana, which was then at its peak and contained everything from the checkered wingtips Powell wore in *The Kennel Club Murder Case* to Powell's personal copy of the shooting script for *Life with Father* to a 1934 letter from Dashiell Hammett congratulating Powell on his interpretation of Nick Charles, which Lazar had managed to obtain from a Powell grand-nephew only minutes before the epistolary buzzards from the University of Texas tried to snap it up. Suzette sold the entire collection, at far less than its value, to that awful Kelso McNair up in Lawndale, who only annexed it to his vast empire of Myrna Loy memorabilia and locked it away in his vault. In retaliation Lazar went down the next morning to their safe-deposit box at Dana Point, removed all six of Suzette's 1958 and '59 Barbie Dolls, and sold them to a collectibles store up in Orange for not quite four thousand dollars, at which point she brought the first suit against him.

"Why is your face turning so red, Bobby?" said Dawn, who must have been all of twenty-two.

"Oh!" he said, not bothering even to sound sincere. "I just remembered. I have an appointment."

"See you, Bobby," said Al.

"See you," he said, but he did not stand up.

"You don't have to keep looking at her, anyway," Al continued reasonably. "You can just look out at Ocean Avenue here, or at my lovely new wife—hi, sweetie—and act as though Suzette's not there."

"I know," Lazar said, smiling at Dawn, then returning his eyes immediately to Suzette. "But I'd like to talk to her. No, really."

So saying, he rose from his chair and walked, as nonchalantly as he could, toward her. He had always been awkward about crossing public space, and could not do it without feeling somehow cheesy and hucksterish, as though he were crossing a makeshift dais in a Legion Hall to accept a diploma from a bogus school of real estate; he worried that his pants were too tight across the seat, that his gait was hitched and dorky, that his hands swung chimpishly at his sides. Suzette was next in line now and studying the menu, even though he could have predicted, still, exactly what she would order: a decaf au lait and a wedge of frittata with two little cups of cucumber salsa. He came up behind her and tapped her on the shoulder; the taps were intended to be devil-may-care and friendly, but of course he overdid them and they came off as the brusque importunities of a man with a bone to pick. Suzette turned around looking more irritated than ever, and when she saw who it was her dazzling green eyes grew tight little furrows at their corners.

"How are you?" said Lazar, daring to leave his hand on her shoulder, where, as though it were approaching c, very quickly it seemed to acquire a great deal of mass. He was so conscious of his hand on her damp, solid shoulder that he missed her first few words and finally had to withdraw it, blushing.

". . . great. Everything's really swell," Suzette was saying, looking down at the place on her shoulder where his hand had just been. Had he laid a freshly boned breast of raw chicken there and then taken it away her expression could not have been more bemused. She turned away. "Hi, Norris," she said to the lesbian woman behind the counter. "Just an espresso."

"On a diet?" Lazar said, feeling his smile tighten.

"Not hungry," she said. "You've gained a few pounds."

"You could be right," he said, and patted his stomach. Since he had thrown Suzette's Borg bathroom scale onto the scrap heap along with her other belongings (thus leaving the apartment all but empty), he had no idea of how much he weighed, and, frankly, as he put it to himself, smiling all the while at his ex-lover, he did not give a rat's ass. "I probably did. You look thinner than ever, really, Suze."

"Here's your espresso," said Norris, smiling oddly at Lazar, as though they were old friends, and he was confused until he remembered that right after Suzette left him he'd run into this Norris at a party in Bluebird Canyon, and they had a short, bitter, drunken conversation about what it felt like when a woman left you, and Lazar impressed her by declaring, sagely, that it felt as though you'd arrived home to find that your dearest and most precious belongings in the world had been sold to a man from Lawndale.

"What about that money you owe me?" he said. The question was halfway out of his mouth before he realized it, and although he appended a hasty ha-ha at the finish, his jaw was clenched and he must have looked as if he was about to slug her.

"Whoa!" said Suzette, stepping neatly around him. "I'm getting out of here, Bobby. Good-bye." She tucked her chin against her chest, dipped her head, and slipped out the door, as though ducking into a rainstorm.

"Wait!" he said. "Suzette!"

She turned toward him as he came out onto the patio,

her shoulders squared, and held him at bay with her cup of espresso coffee.

"I don't have to reckon with you anymore, Bobby Lazar," she said. "Colleen says I've already reckoned with you enough." Colleen was Suzette's therapist. They had seen her together for a while, and Lazar was both scornful and afraid of her and her lingoistic advice.

"I'm sorry," he said. "I'll try to be, um, yielding. I'll yield. I promise. I just—I don't know. How about let's sit down?"

He turned to the table where he'd left Albert, Dawn, and his cup of coffee, and discovered that his friends had stood up and were collecting their shopping bags, putting on their sweaters.

"Are you going?" he said.

"If you two are getting back together," said Albert, "this whole place is going. It's all over. It's the Big One."

"Albert!" said Dawn.

"You're a sick man, Bob," said Albert. He shook Lazar's hand and grinned. "You're sick, and you like sick women."

Lazar cursed him, kissed Dawn on both cheeks, and laughed a reckless laugh.

"Is he drunk or something?" he heard Dawn say before they were out of earshot, and, indeed, as he returned to Suzette's table the world seemed suddenly more stressful and gay, the sky more tinged at its edges with violet.

"Is that Al's new wife?" said Suzette. She waved to them as they headed down the street. "She's pretty, but she needs to work on her thighs."

"I think Al's been working on them," he said.

"Shush," said Suzette.

They sat back and looked at each other warily and with pleasure. The circumstances under which they parted had been so strained and unfriendly and terminal that to find themselves sitting, just like that, at a bright café over two cups of black coffee seemed as thrilling as if they were violating some powerful taboo. They had been warned, begged, and even ordered to stay away from each other by everyone, from their shrinks to their parents to the bench of Orange County itself; yet here they were, in plain view, smiling and smiling. A lot of things had been lacking in their relationship, but unfortunately mutual physical attraction was not one of them, and Lazar could feel that hoary old devouring serpent uncoiling deep in its Darwinian cave.

"It's nice to see you," said Suzette.

"You look pretty," he said. "I like what you've done with your hair. You look like a Millais."

"Thank you," she said, a little tonelessly; she was not quite ready to listen to all his prattle again. She pursed her lips and looked at him in a manner almost surgical, as though about to administer a precise blow with a very small ax. She said, "*Song of the Thin Man* was on last week."

"I know," he said. He was impressed, and oddly touched. "That's pretty daring of you to mention that. Considering."

She set down her coffee cup, firmly, and he caught the flicker of her right biceps. "You got more than I got," she said. "You got six thousand dollars! I got five thousand four hundred and ninety-five. I don't owe you anything."

"I only got four thousand, remember?" he said. He felt himself blushing. "That came out, well, in court—don't you remember? I—well, I lied."

"That's right," she said slowly. She rolled her eyes and bit her lip, remembering. "You lied. Four thousand. They were worth twice that."

"A lot of them were missing hair or limbs," he said.

"You pig!" She gave her head a monosyllabic shake, and the golden curls rustled like a dress. Since she had at one time been known to call him a pig with delicacy and tenderness, this did not immediately alarm Lazar. "You sold my dolls," she said, dreamily, though of course she knew this perfectly well, and had known it for quite some time. Only now, he could see, it was all coming back to her, the memory of the cruel things they had said, of the tired, leering faces of the lawyers, of the acerbic envoi of the county judge dismissing all their suits and countersuits, of the day they had met for the last time in the empty building that had been their restaurant, amid the bare fixtures, the exposed wires, the crumbs of plaster on the floor; of the rancor that from the first had been the constant flower of their love. "You sold their things, too," she remembered. "All of their gowns and pumps and little swimwear."

"I was just trying to get back at you."

"For what? For making sure I at least got something out of all the time I wasted on you?"

"Take it easy, Suze."

"And then to lie about how much you got for them? Four thousand dollars!"

"At first my lawyers instructed me to lie about it," he lied.

"Kravitz! Di Martino! Those sleazy, lizardy, shystery old fat guys! Oh, you pigs!"

Now she was on her feet, and everyone out on the patio had turned with great interest to regard them. He realized, or rather remembered, that he had strayed into dangerous territory here, that Suzette had a passion for making scenes in restaurants. This is how it was, said a voice within Lazar—a gloomy, condemnatory voice—this is what you've been missing. He saw the odd angle at which she was holding her cup of coffee, and he hoped against hope that she did not intend to splash his face with espresso. She was one of those women who like to hurl beverages.

"Don't tell me," he said, despite himself, his voice coated with the most unctuous sarcasm, "you're *reckoning* with me again."

You could see her consulting with herself about trajectories and wind shear and beverage velocity and other such technical considerations—collecting all the necessary data, and courage—and then she let fly. The cup sailed past Lazar's head, and he just had time to begin a tolerant, superior smile, and to uncurl partially the middle finger of his right hand, before the cup bounced off the low wall beside him and ricocheted into his face.

Suzette looked startled for a moment, registering this as one registers an ace in tennis or golf, and then laughed the happy laugh of a lucky shot. As the unmerciful people on the patio applauded—oh, but that made Lazar angry— Suzette turned on her heel and, wearing a maddening smile, strode balletically off the patio of the café, out into the middle of Ocean Avenue. Lazar scrambled up from his chair and went after her, cold coffee running in thin fingers down his cheeks. Neither of them bothered to look where they were going; they trusted, in those last couple of seconds before he caught her and kissed her hollow cheek, that they would not be met by some hurtling bus or other accident.

A MODEL
WORLD

My friend Levine had only a few months to go on his doctoral dissertation, but when, one Sunday afternoon at Acres of Books, he came upon the little black paperback by Dr. Frank J. Kemp, he decided almost immediately to plagiarize it. It was lying at the bottom of a whiskey crate full of old numbers of the *Evergreen Review*, which he had been examining intently because he was trying to get a woman named Betty, who liked the poetry of Gregory Corso, to fall in love with him; he was overexuberant and unlucky in love and had just resolved—for example—to grow some beatnik facial hair. The little book was marked on the outside neither front nor back; it was a plain, black square. Levine picked it up only because he had been lonely for a long time and he idly hoped, on the basis of its anonymous cover, that it might contain salacious material. When he opened it to its title page, he received an indelible shock. "Antarctic Models of Induced Nephokinesis," he read. This was the branch of meteorological engineering he was concerned with in his own researches—in fact, it was the very title he had chosen for his dissertation. Beneath this, Dr. Frank J. Kemp's name was printed, and then the name Satis House—an academic vanity press in Ann Arbor; Levine had seen its discreet advertisement in the back pages of the *Journal of Applied Meteorology*. The date of publication was given, to his astonishment, as 1970, almost twenty years before Levine had had even the dimmest notion of the potential power of Antarctic models— a notion that, despite all his ascetic labor over the past year and a half, remained only partly elucidated. It was a radical conception of nephokinesis even today, and in 1970 sufficiently heterodox, no doubt, to have prevented Kemp from publishing his theory by any other means than paying for it himself.

Levine turned the page and saw that Dr. Kemp had, with a precision that struck Levine as tragic and fine, dedicated his work to the beloved memory of his wife, Jean, 21 May 1900–21 May 1969. Levine imagined the sorrowing, hairless scientist, slumped in a chair beside his wife's hospital bed on a spring day in 1969, his head filled with polar wind. Levine was literally horrified—the hairs on the back of his neck stood erect—at the ignoble fate that had befallen the widower's theory. It was like the horror he had felt, a few weeks earlier, when he had come across the row of bookshelves in the graduate library where the bound dissertations were kept—a thousand white surnames inscribed on a thousand uncracked blue spines, like the grim face of a monument. It was a horror of death, of the doom that awaited all his efforts, and it was this horror, more than anything else—he really was only a few months from finishing—that determined him to commit the mortal sin of Academe.

I had been browsing among the Drama shelves, looking for a copy of anything by Mehmet Monsour, the fashionable Franco-Egyptian theater guru, who was currently serving as guru-in-residence at the university's School of Drama. I was at the beginning of an affair with a guru-prone would-be actress named Jewel, and I had come with Levine to Long Beach only in the hope of finding something that would please her; Levine had been irritable, paranoiac, and unwashed for the past several months, and in general, I confess, I tried to avoid him. When I found nothing at all Franco-Egyptian in the Drama section I went to find Levine, who had said something about going for lunch to a local taqueria that served goat. It was the sort of thing one did with Levine, and I was halfway looking forward to it.

"Levine," I said, "let's go get those tacos." He was slouching against a fire extinguisher at the back of the store, completely absorbed in his reading, eyeglasses slipped down his nose, his mouth open. He suffered from a deviated septum and was a chronic mouth breather. His lank red hair covered one eye. He seemed unpleasantly surprised by what he was reading, as if it were a friend's diary.

"What's that?" I said.

Levine looked up, his face first blank, then irritated; he had forgotten where he was, and with whom, and why.

"That book," I said, with a nod. "You look fascinated. You look scared."

With a sigh Levine stared down at the black book, and bit his lip. "It's going to be my dissertation," he said. "Once I retype it."

"You're going to plagiarize it?"

"I'm going to rescue it," he said. "It and myself."

"Is it on the same subject? There are *other* books on Antarctic models of induced nephokinesis?"

Embarrassed, afraid that I must disapprove of him, he nodded his head. Then, with the childish look of apology he wore when at his most abject—he always looked this way around Betty—he opened the book to its fly and held it out to me.

"It's only seventy-five cents," he said.

He also said that he was too excited to eat anything, particularly goat, and so after he had paid his six bits we walked back to his car. As he pulled onto the freeway, Levine, when he saw that I was not going to censure him, began to expound on his dire plan, which was quite simply to retype Kemp's book on approved thesis paper, in the approved thesis font, within all the prescribed margins; receive his degree; and move to Santa Fe or Taos several months earlier than he had thought possible, where he would set himself up as a maker of ceramic wind chimes. And no one would ever know of his deception, he felt certain of that. He was the only person in the world, besides the author, to have read the book.

"Someone read it," I said. "Or else how did it end up at Acres of Books?"

"Kemp lived in Long Beach. When he died, someone sold off his things, and this ended up at Acres. And there was only one left to sell off, because he burned the rest. In despair."

I stared at him. He was driving as cautiously as ever, both hands on the wheel, never exceeding forty-five miles per hour. He always blamed his meticulous driving on his car, a blue Rambler American that had been his grandmother's, but the truth was that Levine belonged to that large brotherhood of young men, often encountered in Academe, who are obsessively careful about two or three things—the arrangement of socks in their drawers, the alphabetical order of their jazz albums, the proper way to make a Bloody Mary—and slobs in every other regard. In any case he did not look particularly deranged, or desperate, as he wove his fantasies about New Mexico and the scattered estate of Dr. Kemp. He seemed completely certain of everything, in particular of success in his projected crime, and by the time we got back to the graduate-student housing complex, or Gradplex, he even seemed happy. I got him to invite me over to watch the Lakers game on his color television, for the first time in months. He had to retrieve the set from a closet, and, smiling, blow the dust from its screen in a small cloud. I think it was a nice evening for Levine. James Worthy scored thirty-five points, two with a reverse lay-up he sank while on his knees, and at half time Levine went into his bedroom, called Betty, and was successful.

The next morning at eight o'clock, Levine sat down at the kitchen table to begin retyping Kemp's book onto the sheets of archival bond he had purchased, along with three typewriter ribbons, two bottles of Liquid Paper, and a large bag of yogurt-covered raisins, on his way home from Betty's. The acid-free paper had a lifeless, creepy feel, like embalmed flesh, and he felt bad about consigning Kemp's words to it. It was foggy and cool out, and, a rapid typist, he planned to be done by the time the coastal morning burned off and it was glaring, limitless afternoon. There was a pot of coffee on the stove, he had unplugged the telephone, and the package of white raisins sat near at hand. He flexed his fingers, rolled in the first sheet of paper, and began to type.

He soon ran into difficulty, however, when instead of just transmitting Kemp's words mindlessly to his fingertips he made the mistake of reading them and grappling with the concepts they attempted to frame. This slowed his progress considerably, and by the time the sun emerged, around two o'clock, he was still mired in the second chapter, "Modeling on Cationic Residues Found in Austral Solstitial Winds," in which the crux of Kemp's thesis—that the ionized molecules of oxygen frequently found around quickly moving cumulonimbus clouds in the wake of a summer storm on the Ross Ice Shelf presented the likeliest model for nephokinesis—was forcefully argued.

Levine had skimmed through this chapter in the store the day before, paying more attention to the meteorologist's literary style, to see if it at all resembled his own, than to the burden of the prose, and now he found himself entranced. It was a creative, dogged, well-supported, even ingenious argument, and he felt a surge of custodial pride at the boldness of Dr. Kemp's mind. Levine had suspected—it had come to him in a dream, in fact—that Antarctic winds held the key to controlling the dreamy movement of clouds, but he had never really gotten beyond this one intuition. And here it all was! Laid down in charts and statistical tables, with almost a dozen sources that were entirely new to Levine. There was a massive Soviet study of cationic Antarctic winds, undertaken during the International Geophysical Year, which Levine had somehow missed, and there were as well the priceless results of three trips that Dr. Kemp had himself made to the Antarctic, aboard the *Hodge*, in 1963 and 1968. The argument and its advocate were made all the more poignant by the fact that the region in which Kemp had made the crucial measurements was the Bay of Whales, not far from Little America, on the Ross Ice Shelf—a region that had broken off from the continent in 1987 and was now melting. The Bay of Whales was no longer to be found on the map.

("Isn't that going to be a problem with your committee?" I asked him that night as we were on our way to dinner at Professor Baldwin's. "Basing your whole theory on evidence that no longer exists?"

("That's all you guys do," he said—which stung me. I was engaged at that time in the observation of those subatomic particles, such as muons, that lead very short lives. I protested that evanescence itself was in a way the object of my studies— But I'm getting ahead of the story.)

It was nearly sundown when Levine finished his dissertation. His eyes were strained, his back and his neck hurt, but there was a sweet taste in his mouth, for he had regained his faith in the stoic nobility of scientific endeavor, and his regard for the austere beauty of its method. His New Mexican plans, the tinkling of wind chimes in a sonorous breeze, all his months of fruitless research, were forgotten. He had never wanted to be anything but a scientist. He leapt to his feet and dashed out into the gray little Gradplex living room, furnished with only a stereo and a folding aluminum and rubber-lattice lawn chair. His roommate, a graduate student in English, had been expelled from the university earlier in the month, after brawling with a professor over the supposed ties to Benito Mussolini of a female Italian semiotician who was an old girlfriend of the professor's, and now Levine had the place to himself. He lay down on the hard gray carpet and allowed the knuckles of his spine to crack and relax. A breeze blew in from the patio, through the screen door, and ruffled the hair on his damp forehead. Levine thought, as he had not since high school, about the way the breeze was composed of a trillion trillion agitated molecules that he could not see. He thought, with the wondering pedantry of a sixteen-year-old boy, about the way every object around him, including himself, his body, was made of invisible things. He got up, grinning foolishly, and went to the telephone.

Julia Baldwin, the wife of the head of his committee, answered the phone. "What is it?" she said.

"Is Professor Baldwin in?" said Levine, momentarily filled with doubt.

"Just a minute." There was the sound of the receiver rattling as she let it drop. "It's another one of your *god*damned students," he heard her say. Professor Baldwin mumbled something apologetic to her and then said hello.

"I'm sorry to interrupt, Professor Baldwin," said Levine. "It's just—Well, I've been looking into solstitial winds at Ross, and I think—I think I may have stumbled onto something really big. And, well, it kind of scares me, sir, it's so big. I'd kind of like to talk to you about it, if that's all right."

"We're having company, Levine," said Professor Baldwin. "One of my wife's instructors is coming to dinner. What is it, this big, scary thing?"

Levine filled him in briefly on the nature of Kemp's argument for Antarctic models, without of course saying anything about Dr. Kemp. He said that in his opinion a practical method of cloud control was now ten years closer than it had been yesterday. At first Professor Baldwin interjected such comments as "Yes, yes," and "I see," but when Levine had finished he was silent for a long time. Levine could hear Mrs. Baldwin, beautiful Julia, shrieking with laughter in the background.

"Perhaps you'd better come over," said Professor Baldwin. "I'll have to ask Julia. Hold on."

Levine jumped up and down while he waited and watched the last red pennant fade from the evening sky. One of the things he loved best about meteorology was that its domain encompassed sunsets.

"Come in an hour," said Professor Baldwin. "It's fine. In fact, my wife has suggested that you invite your friend Smith. We have a whole salmon."

"Thank you," said Levine. "I'll call him."

It was, of course, this same Julia, or Jewel, Baldwin for whom I had hoped to find that volume of Franco-Egyptian dramatic theory, and I told Levine that I would be more than happy to accompany him.

· · ·

There were coyotes out laughing and looking for pussycat in the foothills above the Facuplex when Levine and I came up the driveway to the Baldwins' house on Froebel Lane. This entire neighborhood, with its skinny new trees on their crutches, its fresh-rolled lawns, its streets named for famous educators, had not been here six months before, and Levine and I had often walked up, carrying our binoculars and a six-pack of beer, to a couple of flat boulders that had stood not far from the present site of the Baldwins' Japanese station wagon. Among a few other things, we shared a soft spot for birds and small animals, although he knew far more about them than I, and we had once been enchanted by the sight of two red rattlesnakes, somewhere in the vicinity of the Baldwins' front door. I reminded Levine of this.

"They were doing it, too," he remembered. "Making love like a couple of snakes."

He rang the doorbell and straightened his necktie. I had told him no one else would have one, but he'd insisted on wearing his. The only tie he possessed, it was at least twenty-five years old, brown, with a vaguely birdlike white figure, inside a pattern of concentric circles, against a grid. He called it his Radar Duck tie, and he generally wore it only on first dates and for court appearances. I was just going to tease him about it for the hundredth time when the door was opened by a large, portly man with very dark skin and gray hair, wearing a bathrobe over a pajama top and sweatpants. The bathrobe had a rodeo motif and was printed with leaping cowboys, lariats, and brands. This was Mehmet Monsour.

"They are having a bitter argument," he said, grinning delightedly and offering us his big brown hand. "Please come in."

We followed Monsour into the tiled living room, sat down at opposite ends of an elderly Danish modern sofa, and folded our hands in our laps. The Baldwins bawled and pleaded in another room. Monsour went to a battered recliner and eased himself backward, taking up a large can of malt liquor and the remote control for the television. Wearing a look of rapt scrutiny, as for the turns of a Berma or a Norma Desmond, he flipped back and forth from a courtroom-simulation program to a talk show on which three transsexuals were discussing the male lives they had abandoned; we'd evidently interrupted his theatrical studies. Like most acting teachers, he was famous chiefly for the whimsical and slightly cruel discipline he imposed on his pupils, and for the unconventional sources of his difficult productions. (Six months later I read in the *Los Angeles Times* a respectful review of Monsour's "harum-scarum" new play, *Divorce Court*.) I had met him only the week before, when Jewel took me to his messy room at the Kon-Tiki Motor Lodge, but he showed not the faintest recognition now, and in fact ignored both Levine and me completely. After five minutes we looked at each other and rose simultaneously to our feet.

"Just tell Professor Baldwin I'll see him tomorrow," said Levine.

"Sure thing," said Mehmet Monsour, waving us brightly away.

We went to the door and were about to go out when Professor Baldwin came to retrieve us. His hands were in the pockets of his gray cardigan, and he was wearing the cool, bored demeanor someone in a store attempts to adopt when he has just broken an expensive item. He looked as though he were going to whistle a little song.

"Where are you going?" he said mildly.

"Oh," said Levine. "Nowhere."

"We just got here," I said. "Just this minute. How are you, Professor Baldwin?"

"We don't have to stay for dinner," said Levine. "We can leave right now." Faced with the substance and strife-haunted eyes of his chairman, and not just his disembodied voice on the phone, Levine felt his feet begin to grow a little cold.

"Nonsense. Julia's just getting dressed. Have you met Mehmet? Met Mehmet. I bet you haven't met Mehmet yet." He gave a small laugh, and I could see that he mistakenly felt the rift in his marriage to have been opened and occupied by Mehmet Monsour, and that he consequently liked to make fun of his visiting, untenured colleague. I felt sorry for Baldwin all at once and wished that I hadn't come. He brought us back into the living room, and then we four sat and watched the television, wondering what it might be like to become a woman. No one spoke. I waited for Jewel to emerge, trying to guess which outfit she would wear. She had a pair of old Levi's I liked, with a rip in the seat which showed bare skin when she bent forward.

"Mr. Smith!" she cried when she appeared at last, in a purple sarong, and took my hand. "Mr. Levine! It's so good to see you!" She attempted, as had her husband, to seem as though she had never in her life raised her voice, let alone in the past quarter of an hour, but her cordiality was brittle, sarcastic, and even a little frightening, as though she were doing Shaw.

"Now, if you gentlemen will just give me twenty minutes," she said, going around to Mehmet Monsour's chair to give his gray head a fond pat. "Everything's almost done."

"Let me help you, Mrs. Baldwin," I said.

"Good," said Professor Baldwin. "Levine, let's you and I sit in my office for a few minutes and talk."

Levine stood instantly, as though summoned to the bench, and followed Professor Baldwin down the hall and into the small room at the back of the house where Baldwin did his revolutionary work on the so-called greenhouse effect. The room looked out over the canyon, toward the mountains, and was furnished with a single cinder-block-and-plank bookcase on which were massed perhaps a hundred books. A much wider plank spanned two sawhorses to make the professor's desk, at which he sat in a Barcelona chair that had belonged to his father-in-law, an architect. There was only a kitchen step stool in the corner for Levine. Although relatively young for a full professor and a laureate of atmospheric science, Baldwin possessed the hard-won virtues of an older man: caution, resignation, frugality. The few strands of black hair on his prematurely lunar head seemed, like his spare office, like his marriage, to be the conscious result of an effort to get by with as little as possible, as though he were preparing for the imminent decline of the biosphere. His only indulgence, aside from a small framed photograph of his wife in a parka on a Falkland island, was his computer—an expensive machine capable of animating color images in three dimensions, which he had bought with some of the money from his MacArthur Fellowship, and which was now running a long, slow simulation of worldwide ozone accretion.

"That's the man my wife is having an affair with," he said, reaching into a cardboard box on the floor beside him. He took out a Baggie filled with marijuana and a small water pipe.

"Smith?" said Levine, and a light went on in his head. I'm afraid I had never told him anything about it.

"Mehmet," said Baldwin, spitting out the last syllable. "Not Smith. It's driving me out of my wits."

Levine didn't know what to say to this. He and his committee chair were not friends. There were one or two graduate students who spent a lot of time in his office on campus, talking about Robert Heinlein and Buckminster Fuller, but they were not Professor Baldwin's friends, either, really. Perhaps Professor Baldwin didn't have any friends.

"Never mind. Forget it." He gave his head a shake. "Tell me about this Ross thing," he said, and lit the pipe. As he inhaled, the professor raised his eyebrows, and lowered them as he blew out. He and Levine passed the pipe in near-silence for several minutes. The room filled with miniature cumulonimbus clouds. Levine looked at the titles of the books on the shelves without registering them until his vacant gaze fell upon a slender black spine at the upper left-hand corner of the bookcase, unmarked, exactly the same height and thickness as the spine of Dr. Kemp's book.

"Oh my," said Levine, exhaling a thick plume.

"What?" said Professor Baldwin. He looked toward the bookcase as if there might be a large spider or rodent crawling across it.

"Were you a student of Dr. Kemp?" Levine could see Baldwin, a little heavier, with hair, standing beside his brave mentor, frost on their faces, against a background of auks and green icebergs. They had been inseparable.

"Dr. Kemp?" Baldwin frowned. "I never heard of him."

This did little to reassure Levine. Even if it were not Dr. Kemp's book on this particular bookshelf, it might as well have been—the book was out there somewhere, waiting; he was going to be found out. He was not in the least surprised, and the sudden renascence in his heart of defeat, of the sense of failure, was almost a relief, as though he had loosened his necktie and unbuttoned his collar. There was no easy way out of the prison of his studies, and he had known this very well until yesterday. His plagiarism had been only an act of self-deception.

"It is Smith," he said, with a feeling of great detachment from the words he spoke.

Professor Baldwin was staring intently at the face of his wristwatch and seemed not to have heard.

"It isn't that Monsour guy," said Levine, abandoning both of us to our fates. "I think it's Smith, sir."

Now the professor looked up at Levine and bit his lip. He was going through the evidence in his mind.

"You could be right," he said. "That sounds feasible."

He replaced the pipe and the plastic bag, carefully, then stood and steadied himself against his desk. On the screen of his computer a model world of weather slowly overheated and drowned.

"What are you going to do?" said Levine.

"I haven't decided yet," said Professor Baldwin. "But something. Him I'm not afraid of." He strode to the door. "A bad student I know how to handle."

"A bad student?" said Levine, rising with a wobble to follow Baldwin out of the cloudy room.

As he switched off the light, Baldwin smiled weakly, as though seeing that his phrase had perhaps not been appropriate.

"You know what I mean," he said.

"Professor Baldwin," said Levine. "What if all of my numbers came out of the Bay of Whales? That wouldn't be good, would it?"

"That wouldn't make any difference at all." He stepped aside in the hall to let Levine pass. "After you," he said.

The party was in its second hour, the bones and oily plates cleared from the table, when Mehmet Monsour was begged to demonstrate one of his famous little games. He and Jewel had done most of the talking during dinner, discussing the theatrical abilities of Bill and Luke and Clothilde and Janet, and particularly of Jewel; malt liquor made Monsour incredibly voluble, it seemed, as with each tall can he came to dominate the conversation more and more, and his stories—how I hate men who tell stories at dinner!—grew increasingly sordid and disturbing. He had been all around the world. Professor Baldwin, Levine, and I were abandoned to our disparate silences. Every time I looked at Baldwin, he was looking at me, beaming at me, really, as though he were in on some happy word of my fortunes, as though I had won some prize. I could hardly eat a thing. Levine nodded his head so intently at the things mentor and pupil were saying that I could see he wasn't listening to a word.

"And so I simply stole it. It was not mine, and it could be of no real practical use to me—you see that," Monsour was saying. He had gotten loud and a little gross in the course of the evening—his bathrobe was all untied and some of the crucial buttons of his pajama top had popped open—and I remembered a piece of advice my father had once given me about never drinking anything that had a number in its brand name except for Vat 69. "While on the contrary, as I look back on it, this radio was her only connection, aside from me, to the outer world. It was precious to her. When I left, she would be cut off completely, as you can see." He shook his head at the memory of this wickedness he had practiced, but with a wistful smile, as though he had long ago forgiven himself.

"I've already heard that story," said Jewel. She had also been drinking malt liquor; the continued adhesion of her sarong was in some doubt. "I told it to you, Baldwin."

"Oh, yeah, I remember," Professor Baldwin said, smiling at me now with perfect fondness. He turned to Mehmet

Monsour. "Why don't you tell these two about that game?
That sounded like a *bear.*"

"Oh, let's play it," said Jewel. She was sitting next to
me, and as she said this she nudged me lightly with her left
elbow. I was certain now that something unpleasant lay in
store for me and certain also, for the first time, that as a
person I meant very little to her. I was just another way of
irritating her husband.

"It is quite simple," said Monsour, whirling on Levine
and catching him off guard. Levine sat up and folded his
hands scholastically in his lap. "In fact, it is hardly a game
at all. We turn out all the lamps." He rose from the table
and gathered about him the flaps of his rootin'-tootin' bathrobe. The candle on the dinner table shed its lone light.
"This is all right, Baldwin?"

"Sure it is," said Baldwin. "Quite all right. I don't think
I'll play, though. I'm no good at this kind of thing."

He looked at Jewel and they blushed like a couple of
lovers.

"Whatever you like. Fine." Monsour sat down again
and picked up his drink. "And now, boys, I would like you
to please tell us." He touched his hands together at the
fingertips and contemplated the resultant structure. "What
is the worst thing you have ever done in your whole, entire
life?" He had asked this question of a thousand students
over the past twenty years, and he paused after the fifth
and ninth words in a way he had discovered to be particularly effective in eliciting a juicy response. "You, Mister,
er—" He nodded his head at Levine. "Levine, I am sorry.
You try first."

In the candlelight my friend's face looked warm and flushed, and although I didn't know the reason, I could see that he was about to unburden himself of success. He uncoiled the tie from around his neck and cast it on the table, then turned to face me, as did Baldwin, Jewel, and Mehmet Monsour.

"After you," he said.

I suppose cuckoldry, charlatanism, and academic corruption are not the only things that could have produced a feeling of unease like the one that now suffused the dinner party. It was as though we all knew that there had been a mild poison in the food, which was now taking effect, and we knew as well who the poisoner was, and we all knew that we knew. It was that sort of unease; the sort generated by a family on the brink of divorce or a team of researchers at work on a new type of death ray. I felt the frank encouragement of Jewel's fingertips on my thigh, pressing me to injure a man who was in some measure eagerly anticipating his injury, but her face, like her husband's and Monsour's and Levine's, and, I imagine, like my own, was uncertain and a little pinched.

Fortunately I had the presence of mind to tell the truth. I told them that as a child I had had a reputation for honesty and probity of which I felt miserably undeserving. I said, shame already beginning to mount in my belly, that one summer evening I had gone barefoot down the sidewalk in our deserted neighborhood, set free from the dinner table earlier than anyone else. I had heard a distant lawnmower, a sprinkler, TV gunfire. I had passed the garage of a friend named Mike, who just that day, I knew, had been given a new toy car; the garage door was raised and I could see a card table on which stood some jars of model paint, a half-constructed model bomber, and the new red Matchbox. For no particular reason at all I grabbed a brush and a jar of silver paint and blotted out the windshield and rear window of the toy, threw it to the ground, stepped on it, and then ran home. The horrible part had been afterward, when I returned to Mike's house to find all the neighborhood children standing around denying that they had been vandals. "Smith didn't do it," Mike's older brother had said. "That's for sure, anyway." That night as I got ready for bed I had discovered two streaks of glitter on the sole of my foot.

"You're making it up," said Mehmet Monsour, with a mysterious, Nilotic laugh. "Well done."

"I didn't believe it," said Jewel. She stood up from the table and began to clear the rest of the dishes.

"Neither did I," said Baldwin, and I suddenly found myself free of his unbearable look of kindness.

"What about me?" said Levine.

"I'm so bored!" said Monsour in a cheery voice, as though announcing his intention to take a brisk postprandial swim. He rose from the table and went back to the television.

I was surprised, as I took my leave of Monsour that evening, when he asked me to attend his next Grand Seminar, at a local ice rink, later in the month—so surprised that I consented. Monsour's interest in me may have irked Jewel; she stopped calling. I guess she had no more real use for me, if she'd ever had any. She did not attend the seminar, and I haven't seen her for a long time. At the ice rink, for forty-eight hours during which we imitated various animals, fasted, shrieked, and held our water, I began to learn something of the aboriginal connection between anguish and entertainment. The whole thing was a grueling and silly but nonetheless eye-opening experience, and I guess I have to credit Monsour with whatever success I have since found on the stage and even, if this deal with Lucifex Pictures goes through, on the silver screen. I've written a screenplay, as a vehicle for myself, based on the heroic life of Werner Heisenberg. I haven't completely abandoned physics, you see. Of course I know what everyone says about Hollywood, and sometimes it is a little disheartening to think of making my way in a pit of savage vipers, but I have no reason not to consider myself equal to the task. As for Levine, his dissertation caused an uproar in the field after its second chapter was published in *JAM*. He dropped right into the tenure track at Caltech, with access to a huge laboratory and a twelve-million-dollar Cray computer, and when I went up to Pasadena the other day he told me, with a note of awe and delight in his voice, that the human race is now only a few years away, by most reckonings, from total dominion over the clouds.

BLUMENTHAL

ON THE AIR

Anglophones of Paris, ladies and gentlemen, fellow Americans in exile or on vacation or both, I have a wife; and she has her green card. We live beside the most beautiful cemetery in the world. When we walk along the quiet streets of Père-Lachaise, climb all the staircases to its highest tombs, stand before the small stone palace that holds the bones of a Russian princess, sometimes Roksana talks sweetly and kisses me on my ear or fingertip, and for a second we'll seem married and almost normal. But in any other part of Paris, and in several parts of the United States, I am merely the man who is making her a citizen, and she will hardly look my way. Roksana is Iranian—or Persian, as she prefers to say—big and black-haired; her lips and lashes are thick and dark; she can beat me up. She is the most beautiful woman I've ever known, but when she's angry or seized by Persian lust, something enters her face and she gets to looking savage, ancient, one quarter ape.

I was playing records in Dallas, working for an FM station far down on the left-hand side of your radio dial, hanging around with the kind of people who have imperiled foreigners as friends, when I heard that an Iranian woman

of iron will and countenance was looking for a husband. I
met her at a party, watched her drink a whiskey, and, as
Roksana spoke unwillingly of her battles, old and new, with
secret police and landlords, zealots and bureaucrats, spoke
of the loss of her father, of the terrible tedium of home-
lessness in a tone neither self-pitying nor angry, I admired
her. Initially, it was only that—a marriage of admiration
and desperation, made for neither money nor love. Under
the gaze of the I.N.S., the love police, we planned to live
together, intimately perhaps, for the three years it would
take her to become a citizen, divorce, and afterward main-
tain nothing more than a strange, inexplicable friendship.
Had I not breached our contract by actually falling in love,
we would still be in Texas, counting the days, but here we
are, in the capital of France, waiting for her heart, or mine,
to undertake a change.

So now, every Saturday from eight to midnight I play
records here on La Voix du Brouillard, and talk about Los
Angeles in school French, because certain Parisians are
crazy for L.A., where my brother, Calvin, is an Artists and
Repertoire man for Capitol Records. Once a week he sends
me an account of his previous seven days of living on the
edge, of parties, of massive car accidents, of billiard-ball
trysts with models and waitresses, knocking into them and
then spinning off into some other corner of the city. I
translate his letters and read them over the air, in a Rod
Serling voice (tricky in French). I have fans; girls call me
up and, on the air, promise me rendezvous and the round
parts of their bodies, and so on. Guys call to request songs,
to tell me about their pilgrimages to southern California in

1969 or 1979, the wild blondes they met there, *le délire californien*, and so on.

Tonight Roksana calls after I play a song for her. She says thank you, very politely, and we don't chat. I picture her sitting at the table with the radio and the telephone, in her men's underwear, eating a plate of boiled meat or a five-ton slab of some Iranian dessert, listening to the sound of my voice speaking in a language she doesn't know. When I picture this, I am filled with love and hopelessness. Paris seemed like a good idea when I was hopeless in New York, the way New York did when I was hopeless in Dallas, but it hasn't worked even the slightest charm, and Roksana's tremendous heart slumbers on. I do not even have her thanks. "You should have charged me," she has said, twice. "I would have paid."

After she hangs up, I put on "Sister Ray," because it's seventeen minutes long, and I go to stand in the street outside the studio and smoke three cigarettes end to end. No one else is in the little studio at this hour, and the thought of the stylus drawing nearer and nearer to the emptiness after the last groove of the song, without me there to make the segue, thrills me and keeps me from thinking about everything else. And then when I am thrilled enough, I drop the third cigarette and rush back into the studio, with the stumbling, happy urgency of someone who has heard the milk on the stove begin to boil over. I play this game pretty often. Sometimes I make it, sometimes there's a terrible pause.

At midnight I shake hands with Jean-Marc, le Jazz-Maniac, who's on his way in for his shift. Then I'm out and I echo along the street to the Métro and clatter down onto the empty platform. At the foot of an advertisement for a new American film, someone has scrawled a tangle of Farsi, a long, descending statement followed by three tiny exclamation points, and it looks to me like the notation for a difficult passage of music, a decrescendo. I catch the next-to-last train home and ride alone in the fluorescence the whole slow way. I've read all the advertisements, all the safety warnings and every damn word of French between the Europe and the Père-Lachaise stations a hundred times, and now reading them again makes me jumpy, impatient. I'm in a hurry because it's late and we still have to pack for our trip to Brittany tomorrow. And when I get home, Roksana's stretched out on the sofa with her eyes wide open and the two suitcases are lying empty on the living-room floor.

"Roksana," I say, "I saw some Persian graffiti in the Métro again tonight."

"I didn't write it," she says.

"Come on, let's talk. Tell me some more about Iran."

We've finished packing and we're on the sofa, and I draw her big head down onto my lap; I hold it there. Her hair is always cool to the touch. The light in the living room, dim and pink through the heavy shade on the only lamp, tends to put us to sleep anyway, and now it's 3 A.M.; Roksana is going under, eyelids fluttering. Every so often she stirs and struggles to free her hair from my twining fingers. She stiffens her neck, and against my thigh I feel the hardness of the muscles of her back. Now that I've mentioned Iran, she springs up and goes to perch on the other end of the sofa, black eyes, no nonsense. My lap feels cold.

"What about Iran?" she says. "Let's not."

"No, please." I don't really want to talk about Iran, either. We've had this conversation a thousand times before, but what else is there? About the things someone would write on an advertisement in the Métro. "I don't know. The shah, the ayatollah."

"Tell me what you think," she says, barely, and yawns, and there again are the three gold teeth I bought for her. I had heard that toothache can cause profound, moral sadness.

"As far as I could see, um, the shah was an asshole and they threw him out, but he died anyway. And then the ayatollah came in, and he's an asshole, too. And a bunch of sweaty guys were running around throwing Coke cans and setting American flags on fire."

"That's it," she says. She stands up, I watch her black knit dress gather around her hips, then fall, one instant of yellow boxers. "I'm going to bed. Goodnight."

Many things fill the distance between me and Roksana, and one of them is the nation of Iran. If you look at a map, I am the Caspian Sea, and she is the Persian Gulf. Once upon a time, I suppose, the whole place was underwater.

Roksana hoists our suitcases and we follow Hervé Heugel down onto the platform at Le Pouliguen, where we stand waiting for his mother or his father, I'm not sure which, to take us to the Heugel manor, or *château*, as Hervé calls it. I've known Hervé for about a month. He lives in our neighborhood in Paris and takes his morning coffee around the corner from our apartment, at the Voltaire, where one day he spotted my accent and my Velvet Underground T-shirt and, after I gave him the money for a croissant, became my friend. Though he looks kind of intellectual and severe—big forehead, pointy chin, rimless glasses, and a crew cut—it turns out that he has no interests other than the usual nonintellectual ones. He loves to laugh and to swear in English—the only English he knows. He and Roksana don't like each other very much, although neither would ever say so. They can barely speak to each other, anyway. Hervé is arrogant, callous, and I often feel myself getting on his nerves, but he knows his garage bands of the late sixties, and he knows the city, and sometimes he drives me around Paris on the back of his motor scooter, his thin scarf flapping in my face. I think that if I met someone like Hervé in America, I wouldn't make friends with him, but there are no people like him in America. And, anyway, friendship is different in another language; a foreign friend doesn't have to understand what you feel, and I don't expect it. It's enough if he understands what you just said.

We can smell the sea now, and I look around eagerly at the tiny cars, the embracing families, the ancient candy machine rusting next to the men's room, and at the low brown houses and scrub fields that surround the train station.

"She is there," says Hervé. He pushes his stern little glasses up his nose, drops his Adidas duffel. When his mother reaches us, he takes her in his arms, gets it on both cheeks, and then presents us. His mother is short, a bit wrinkled but fine-featured, with motionless hair.

"Ah, the little Americans," she says uncertainly. "Brine."

"Brian. Brian Blumenthal," says Hervé, fairly well. "And—Roksana—Khairzada."

"Brine," says Madame Heugel, and she takes my hand, a complex expression on her face—a smile-frown, or a polite sneer. Or just a face that is uncomfortable with our names, and with our presence, and with my wife, and with her own son. whom, I know, she considers lazy, sly, and overly fond of Americans, particularly of American girls.

She asks her son if we speak French; I answer for both of us. "I do, my wife regrets that she doesn't." Then Hervé takes her arm and off they go, speaking French, and we follow.

"She hates me," Roksana says quietly.

"No, she doesn't. Why do you say that?"

"It's all right, I don't care. She can hate me."

I try to pull her to me, and I'm about to say again those three helpless words when she stops short.

"Look," she says.

Behind the scratched display window of the candy machine is a brand of chocolate bar with an English name: Big Nuts. Roksana laughs. I buy one and put it in my pocket, and when we reach the Heugel Renault, I am still smiling.

"Oh, what beautiful teeth," says Madame Heugel.

"Yes, they're like that—American teeth," says Hervé.

We eat outside, at a long table, and lunch is a mountain of steamed shrimp, a stacked cord of fresh asparagus, cider, and bread. Hervé's father, who looks like Hervé—thin with a large head and a sharp nose—tells us in French about his trip to New York City in 1968. I am delighted by his account of a misadventure in "les Bronx," and everything goes well until I notice that my plate is the only one on which mounts a pile of tails, shells, rosy filaments, and shrimp heads; Hervé and his parents are eating the entire shrimp, unpeeled. Roksana will not eat shrimp.

"No one told me what kind of a neighborhood I would have to walk through to get to the Cloisters," says Monsieur Heugel, struggling with the word. He has shot five small fowl that morning and seems to be in fine spirits; I saw the brown and iridescent-green pile of birds on the kitchen table. "Harlem! Think of that! Full of blacks! Did I care?"

"Yes," Hervé says.

"No, I did not. I walked right through. On my way home I had an appetite, I stopped at a little coffee shop, I bought a sandwich, I sat right down on the curb, in Harlem, and ate it. No one bothered me." He smiles at his wife, who probably hears this story every time the Heugels feed an American, and she smiles and reaches to move his sleeve out of the butter dish. "I have nothing against blacks, you see."

"Since when?" Hervé turns to me. "He's completely prejudiced against blacks. Blacks and Arabs."

Right away he puts an embarrassed hand to his mouth, and we all turn to look at Roksana—myself included, which makes me ashamed—who has no idea of what's been said and continues calmly to eat her asparagus and bread, eyes to her plate. While Monsieur Heugel protests that he has known several Arabs who were very worthwhile fellows and, it must be said, skilled businessmen, and Hervé snorts and puts away fistfuls of shrimp, I push back my chair.

Our table is spread in the grassy *clos* between two of the estate's several houses. On my right is an ivy-covered stone building with a turret, five chimneys, and fabulous eaves—the house of Hervé's family; on my left, across the lawn, is one of the larger outbuildings, a brown barn that has been converted into a guesthouse. All around our table are bees and butterflies and giant oaks, the air smells lightly of manure and salt, and across from me, in the distance behind Monsieur Heugel, is the bay, filled with sails. I watch Roksana chew, closed, dark, mute, immovable, and I think: I am a fool.

"Oh, the little American," says Madame Heugel, pointing delicately with her fork at my plate. "He will not eat the heads!"

They laugh, and Roksana looks up.

"In America," I say, "it's unlucky to eat them." I fold another buttery stalk of asparagus into my mouth. The Heugels shoot another round of glances at my staring wife.

"Monsieur Heugel," I say, "how many centuries has this manor been in your family?"

"Hervé's grandfather purchased the manor in 1948," says Madame Heugel.

Everyone laughs much louder this time. Roksana looks up again, her face blank, her jaw working, and for one moment, and for the first time, I feel like striking her.

I excuse myself, leaving Roksana to sit at their table, to suck up all their joy and conversation like a black hole. I hate all of them.

Upstairs, I sit in the tub and hold the hand nozzle over my head for a few minutes, showering off the train ride and the strange conversation, which, after all, I may have misunderstood. Then I go back into the bedroom the Heugels have given us, which smells of cedar. With a towel on my head I step over to one of the lozenge-shaped windows and look outside, onto the yard, where the table is still covered with the wreckage of lunch and where Hervé and his father drink Calvados from little glasses. Roksana and Hervé's mother have disappeared, perhaps into the house, and I have this brief, stupid, happy fantasy of the two of them doing the dishes together, working in smooth and wordless concert.

When I take from my suitcase the new dress shirt, white with coral pinstripes, that I bought specially at an outlet store in the rue du Commerce, because Hervé had promised to take us to a Breton club where the women would go wild over my accent, the shirt is wrinkled and my shaving cream has exploded all across the collar. I sit down on the bed, looking for a long time at the pale blue smear of foam and trying to remember the word for clothes iron.

The stairs creak. Roksana's face is in the doorway for half a second, and I think she's coming into the bedroom. I toss aside the spoiled shirt, but she turns and I hear her start to creak back downstairs. I shut my eyes. "Roksana."

Plates in the kitchen, laughter outside.

"I need to be alone."

"Please come here."

When I open my eyes she's in the doorway again. This time I see the anger on her face, and before the words come out of her mouth I know, with a rush of bent happiness, that we're going to have a fight, after a year and a half of wedlock as empty and quiet as a dark theater.

"I want to leave," she says, coming into the room and slamming the door behind her. "I'm not welcome here. You stay. They like you."

"You're as welcome as you choose to be."

"No. Bullshit. They were laughing. They were laughing at me. I could tell. You were laughing at me, you bastard."

"You bitch."

I'm still sitting down, and Roksana steps so close to me now that the tips of her pointed black shoes come down, hard, on my toes. She throws a shadow across me.

"Please, don't," I say.

"I don't know why I'm here."

"You're here because it's Bastille Day. You're here to have fun. Ouch! Can't you ever have fun?"

Roksana looks down upon me, her eyes perfectly dry and black, and says that she hates fun more than anything else in this world, and I see that I misunderstood her when she said she didn't know why she was here, because I thought that by "here" she just meant in Brittany.

"You sound like Khomeini," I say, trying to slide my pinched feet out from under her shoes, and feeling somehow offended, as though I were responsible for all of us, and for the fireworks and feast days and surfeits of the entire fun hemisphere. I manage to free my feet, but now she grabs me by the ears and pulls, and it hurts.

"What do you know about Khomeini? What do you know about me? I am not fun. Do you think to run away from Iran was fun? From my mother? From the bodies of my family?"

"I'm sorry," I say, still angry. "Fine. Go. Go back. All I have to do is say the word to Mr. Immigration and you can go right back to the land of seriousness."

"You won't."

"I might," I say, and think, well, I could. But I can't stand the frightened, stubborn way she has narrowed her eyes or the way the room and the air between us seems filled with the cheesy smell of blackmail. I look down and my gaze falls upon the blue on my shirt collar. "You said I should have charged you. I'm charging you now."

There is no human sound from downstairs, which means, I suppose, that the Heugels have been listening to our raised foreign voices. Roksana sits down beside me, rubbing softly now at the sides of my head. Her shoulders droop, and her little pink earrings swing back and forth like the clappers of two invisible bells.

"What is Bastille Day, anyway?"

"It's like the Fourth of July."

"Beer and noise," says my wife, the ayatollah of love, remembering last year in Texas with an unanswerable frown. This year, for us, there was no Fourth of July. I woke up on the fifth, feeling guilty and strange for having forgotten, and went alone to the Burger King on the Champs-Elysées.

"I'm sorry, Brian Blumenthal," she says at last. "I can't do it."

Dinner, from discussion to drinks to preparation, from further drinks to further discussion to eating, from the time we passed around five kinds of cheese for dessert to the time we wearily threw down our napkins and drank a bit more, took five hours, and now, stunned by food, I'm drifting with Hervé and his family along the heights of the cliff town of Kerguen, where we've come to see the fireworks. Roksana has stayed behind. The last orange light of the day flows across the houses and across the faces of the Heugels, and in the coolness, the clouds of gnats and fireflies and the smell of the nearby farms grow denser. I've drunk too much brandy, understood too little talk, and, as night falls around us, I feel deaf and blind. Only my nose is alive, with mown fields, livestock, low tide.

The townspeople are all out-of-doors, strolling from the *place* to the cliff's edge and back, shaking hands, waiting for the display to begin; and the children and careful fathers fill the wait with match flares, loud firecracker pops and whistles and laughter, just as in the United States. But there's that difference I always feel in French crowds, a lack of excitement that is not exactly boredom, but like an air of age, of deep habit, even among the children, as though these same five hundred people have been coming to stand and talk together forever and ever. A platform for dancing has been built, and it stands empty and brightly lighted at one end of the *place*, surrounded by loudspeakers and tricolors.

We hear the first commanding bang from across the inlet and lift our eyes. The fireworks are fireworks; they spray and glitter and lightly move me like every display of fireworks I have seen in every July I remember, and lingering octopi of smoke float over our heads. During the applause and cries after the long last outburst, Hervé takes my arm and pulls me down along the cliffs, where we kick stones out into the water, and he surprises me by asking if there is anything wrong. I try to find the French for it; I tell him about all the useless gold in her downturned mouth.

Hervé says, "Oh la la," which I didn't think Frenchmen ever really said; and in a language that is always wistful, it is the most wistful phrase that I have heard, and I start to cry.

And then he says, "Why did you marry her?," although he already knows the practical and bureaucratic answer to this question.

We walk farther and stand high above the water on the last two feet of Kerguen. "She is not pretty. *Elle a une drôle de tête.* And she is so gloomy, it must be said. No, it's a good thing you did, perhaps. I see that. But it's an arrangement. No? And she understands. You are the one who makes the mess."

There are a few stray firecrackers, then a loud *whomp*, then laughter.

"Sometimes," he says, "it irritates me to see you made a fool."

"Thank you," I say.

"But then I remember that you're an American."

They start the music down in the *place,* and before I can say anything, Hervé moves slowly back away from the edge, and looks down on the town. I go to stand beside him, and we watch the distant dancing to a French song that sounds like it's from the fifties, a ballad about a girl named Aline. The kids hold each other and rock, barely, from foot to foot.

"Ah, *le slow,*" says Hervé, tying the sleeves of his sweater more firmly around his neck. "This is an ancient song. It gives me nostalgia, this music."

"Me, too," I say.

"Do you dance with your wife?"

"I could never get my arms all the way around her," I say.

We laugh. I sniffle and wipe my nose, and I'm on the point of asking him for advice, for the cool, sober shrug of French counsel that will brace me for the act of surrendering up my wife, when the wind shifts, and the reckless note of the saxophone is carried off to the east. In the sudden absence of music, it comes to me that Hervé has already told me what to do, and that I must follow, until the finish, the foolish policy of all my hopeless race.

SMOKE

———————

It was a frigid May morning at the end of a freak cold snap that killed all the daffodils on the lawns of the churches of Pittsburgh. Matt Magee sat in the front seat of his old red Metropolitan, struggling with the French cuffs of his best shirt. This was a deliberate and calm struggle. He did not relish the prospect of Drinkwater's funeral, and he was in no hurry to go in. He had already sat and fiddled and listened to the radio and rubbed lovingly at his left shoulder for ten minutes in the parking lot of St. Stephen's, watching the other mourners and the media arrive. Magee was not all that young anymore, and it seemed to him that he had been to a lot of funerals.

On the evening that Eli Drinkwater wrecked his Fleetwood out on Mt. Nebo Road, Magee had been sent down to Buffalo after losing his third consecutive start, in the second inning, when he got a fastball up to a good right-handed hitter with the bases loaded and nobody out. He'd walked two batters and hit a third on the elbow, and then he had thrown the bad pitch after shaking off Drinkwater's sign for a slider, because he was so nervous about walking in a run.

Eli Drinkwater had been a scholarly catcher, a redoubt-able batsman, and a kind, affectionate person, but as Magee lost his stuff their friendship had deteriorated into the oc-casional beer at the Post Tavern and terse expressions of pity and shame. Little Coleman Drinkwater was Magee's godson, but he hadn't seen the boy in nearly four years. It was the necessity of encountering Drinkwater's widow and son at the funeral, along with his erstwhile teammates, that kept Magee hunched over behind the wheel of his car in an empty corner of the church parking lot, rolling his cuffs and unrolling them, as the car filled with the varied ex-halations of his body. For eleven and a half hours now, he'd been working on a quart of Teacher's. He was not attempting to get roaring drunk, or to assuage his profes-sional disgrace and the sorrow of Drinkwater's death, but with care and a method to poison himself. It was not only from Drinkwater that he had drifted apart in recent years; he seemed to have simply drifted apart, like a puff of breath. He was five years past his best season, and his light was on the verge of winking out.

At last Magee started to shiver in the cold. He fastened his pink tourmaline cuff links, turned off the radio, and climbed out of the car. He was nearly six feet five, and it always gave other people a good deal of pleasure to watch him unfold himself out of the tiny Metropolitan. According to the settlement of his divorce from his wife, Elaine, he had ended up with it, even though it had been hers before. Elaine had ended up with everything else. Thanks to a bad investment Magee had made in an ill-fated chain of base-ball-themed, combination laundromat-and-crabhouses, this consisted of less than seventy-one thousand dollars, a king-size mobile home in Monroeville with a dish and a Jacuzzi bathtub, and a five-year-old Shar-Pei with colitis. Magee retrieved his sober charcoal suit jacket and navy tie from the minute rear bench of the Metropolitan and slowly knotted the necktie. The tie had white clocks on it, and the suit was flecked with a paler gray. He had lost his overcoat—a Hart Schaffner & Marx—on the flight down to Florida that spring, and had hoped he wouldn't be needing one again. Just before Magee slammed the car door, he paused a moment to study his two small suitcases, side by side on the passenger seat, and allowed himself to imagine carrying them to any one of a thousand destinations other than Buffalo, New York. Then he checked his hair in the window, patted it in two places, and headed across the parking lot toward the handsome stone church.

It was warm inside St. Stephen's, and there was a wan smell of woolens and paper-whites and old furniture polish. Magee took up a place behind the last row of pews, over by the far wall, among some reporters he knew well enough to hope that they would not be embarrassed to see him. The arrangements for the funeral had been made without fanfare, and although the church was filled from front to back, there were still not as many people as Magee had expected. The minister, a handsome old man in a gilded chasuble, murmured out over the scattered heads of Drinkwater's family and teammates. There was to be a memorial ceremony later in the week which ought to pack them in. By then the newspaper eulogies would have worked their way past shock and fond anecdote and begun to put the numbers together, and people would see what they had lost. Drinkwater had led the league in home runs the past two years, and his on-base average over that period was .415. He had walked three times as often as he struck out, and had last year broken the season record for bases stolen by a catcher—not that this had been all that difficult. The lifetime won-lost percentage for games he had caught, which to Magee's mind was the most important statistic of all, was close to .600; had he not been required to catch most of the fifty-odd games Magee had lost during that period, it would have been even better. Drinkwater had been cut down in his prime, all right. And that was what the numbers would show.

"Too bad it couldn't have been you instead of him," said a gravelly female voice at his ear. He turned, startled at hearing his own thought echoed aloud. It was Beryl Zmuda, in a fur coat, and she was only kidding, in her gravelly way. Beryl was a sports columnist for the Erie morning paper, and she had known Magee ever since Magee had come up in that city, with the Cardinals organization. A laudatory article by Beryl, written after Magee's first professional shutout, had gotten things rolling for him eleven years before. In that game Magee had struck out nine batters in a row and made the last out himself by bare-handing a line drive. No one was more disappointed by what had become of Magee's career than Beryl Zmuda.

"Hey, Ber," said Magee in a whisper. "When do I get to go to your funeral?"

"It was last year. You missed it." She did not trouble to whisper. She wore a myrtle-green hat with a heron feather which he had seen many times before. "You look terrible. But as usual that's a lovely suit."

"Thanks."

They shook hands, and then Magee bent down to kiss her. She sniffled and leaned forward to accept his kiss. Her pointed nose was still red from the cold, and he found her cheeks a little wet. The sable coat felt delightful and smelled both of warm fur and of Quelques Fleurs, and he had to force himself to let go of her. They had slept together for two months during the minor-league season of 1979, and Magee still held a fond regard for her. Her uncle had been a wartime pitcher for the St. Louis Browns; she knew baseball, especially pitchers, and she could write a nice line. Because of her name, she favored the color green, and under the coat her funeral suit was a worn gabardine the somber hue of winter seawater.

"What a shame it is," he said, wiping at his own eyes. Magee was a sucker for weeping women, and lachrymose when he had been drinking.

"He had a great April," said Beryl. Her Pittsburgh accent was flat and angular. She had fifteen years on Magee, and it was starting to tell. Her hair, blond as an ashwood bat, was entirely the product of technology now, and her face was looking papery and translucent and pinched at the corners. But she still had nice legs, with the pomaceous calves of a Pittsburgh girl. She had been raised on the steep staircases of Mt. Washington.

"He did," said Magee. "Three-thirty-one with seven home runs and eighteen ribbies."

"Hey, how about you?" She looked him up and down

as though he had just gotten out of the hospital. "How's the arm?"

He shrugged; the arm was fine. Magee had a problem with his mechanics. He had become balky and as wild as a loose fire hose. Although on the hill he felt the same as he had since the age of fourteen, jangling and irritable and clearheaded, some invisible element of his delivery had changed. The coaches felt that it was the fault of his right foot, which seemed to have grown half a shoe size in recent years. Whatever the cause, he could no longer find what Eli Drinkwater had called the wormhole. Drinkwater had picked up this term from Dr. Carl Sagan's television program. A pitched ball passing through the wormhole disappeared for an instant and then reappeared somewhere else entirely, at once right on target and nowhere near where it ought to be, halfway across the galaxy, right on the edge of the black. Magee's repeated, multiseasonal failure to find the wormhole had bred fear, and fear caution; he had undergone some horrendous shellings.

"It's fine," said Magee, rubbing at his left shoulder. "I'm going up to Buffalo this afternoon. Right after this." He nodded in the general direction of the altar, before which sat the closed casket that held the body of Eli Drinkwater. It was a fancy black casket, whose size and finish and trim recalled those of the massive American automobiles its occupant had preferred.

The pastor finished his bit, and Gamble Wicklow, the Pittsburgh manager, rose to his feet and approached the pulpit. He was an eloquent speaker with a degree in law from Fordham—his sending down of Magee had been a masterpiece of regret and paternal solicitude—but he looked tired and elderly today. Magee could not make out what he was saying. Gamble had been sitting beside Roxille Drinkwater, in the foremost pew, and now there was a gap between Roxille and little Coleman. The sight of this gap was poignant, and Magee looked away.

"Will you look at that," said Beryl. She went up on tiptoe to get a clearer view.

"I can't," said Magee.

"Look how Roxille's looking at that casket."

The reporters on either side of them, saddened, serious as the occasion required, were still rapacious and insatiable. They turned toward the grieving widow with the simultaneity of starlings taking wing. There was indeed something odd in the face and the posture of Roxille Drinkwater. Roxille was a pretty woman, a little heavy. Her russet hair was pulled tightly against her head and tied at the back. She wore no veil, and the look in her eyes was angry and complicated, but Magee thought he recognized it. Her husband had blown away, out of her life, like an empty wrapper, like a cloud of smoke. She was wondering how she could ever have thought he was real. As Magee watched she began to rock a little in the pew, back and forth. It was hardly noticeable at first, but as Wicklow's voice rose to praise her dead husband for his constancy and steadiness, and to foretell the endurance of his presence in the game, Roxille's rocking gathered force, and Magee knew he would have to do something.

Once, on an airplane, Magee had seen Roxille lose it.

It had been during a night flight from New York, where Drinkwater had gone to collect an award, to Pittsburgh, aboard a careering, rattling, moaning little two-propeller plane. Roxille had begun by rocking in her seat, rocking and staring into the darkness outside the window of the plane. She had finished by shrieking and praying aloud, and then slapping a stewardess who attempted to calm her down. Now the people sitting in the pews around Roxille exchanged worried looks. Joey Puppo, the G.M., was frowning, and glancing frequently toward the reporters, who had begun to mutter and click their tongues. Magee saw that she intended, whether she knew it or not, to hurl herself across the gleaming black lid of the coffin.

"She won't do it," said Beryl, in a voice that just qualified as a whisper. She had little esteem for other women, in particular for baseball wives.

"This is a funeral," said a television sports reporter, a former outfielder named Leon Lamartine who once at Wrigley had knocked one of Magee's sliders—a high, hard one that was not quite hard enough—out onto Waveland Avenue, under a rosebush and into pictures that were shown on national TV. His tone seemed to imply not that decorum would prevent Roxille from doing something outrageous but that anything was possible at funerals.

"Hey, c'mon, you guys," said Magee. "Keep it down." But he cracked his knuckles and worked his shoulder blades a couple of times, just in case.

Gamble Wicklow was winding down now. His chin had settled into his chest, and he was commending the departed soul of Eli Drinkwater to the Man in charge of putting together the Great Roster in the Sky. Roxille licked her lips. Her eyelids fluttered. She reached out tentatively toward the stylish coffin. Three dozen cameras and recording devices turned upon her. Magee moved.

"Where you going, Matty?" said Beryl, whirling. "Oh, my. Oh, my."

". . . now that Eli Drinkwater has forever become, as I think we may truly say, All-Star," said Gamble Wicklow, putting a period to his elegy with a sad smile.

"I told you," Leon Lamartine said, pointing.

Magee had delayed too long—his timing was irrevocably off—and his initial smooth glide down the aisle toward the first pew became a two-way foot race as Gamble stepped down from the pulpit. Magee was forced to run while pretending that he was still walking, all the time trying to keep his head down and remain inconspicuous. The result was an unintentional but skilled approximation of the gait of Groucho Marx. Only the fact that Gamble and the next eulogist collided by the entrance to the chancel allowed Magee to occupy Gamble's place in the pew. Magee put his left arm around Roxille, as though to comfort her, and wrestled her back into her seat.

"Take it easy," said Magee in his softest voice.

When Gamble Wicklow saw that Magee had usurped his seat, he frowned, gave an odd little wave, then turned and trudged managerially up the aisle. His suit was of old tweed and fit him ill. The nave of St. Stephen's filled with rumor and alarm and a faint, funereal laughter.

"Magee. Oh, Magee. What in the hell am I going to do?" Roxille said quietly. Her voice was almost inaudible when she said the word "hell." Her eyes were bloodshot and lively. She was not really looking at Magee but around him, at her son, who had turned and clambered to his knees in the pew to see what was going on back there among the cameras. Coleman had grown to be a good-looking little boy, long-limbed and as dark as his father. His hair had been cut very short, and, according to the fashion, a design had been carved into the stubble at the side of his head; it looked like a couple of eyeballs.

Magee put his hand on Roxille's forearm. She had on an expensive-looking black knit dress with a black lace collar and noticeable gores. She smelled of Castile soap.

"I don't know, Roxie," he said. He blushed. He felt very out of place, here in the front row, and he was ashamed to have gone so long without visiting or speaking to her, but he was glad that he had kept her off national TV. "You'll get along."

Roxille shuddered and took a deep breath. She closed her wild eyes and then opened them carefully. The minister had regained the pulpit and managed, by dint of looking pale and disappointed, to quiet the murmuring. He then introduced the next eulogist, a writer from *Sports Illustrated*. This man had started out working at the same Erie newspaper as Beryl, and not all that long ago. He was talented and he had done well for himself. Beryl hated him, in a good-humored way, and this led Magee to wonder why he had not hated Eli Drinkwater, whose fortunes had begun to rise so soon after Magee lost sight of the wormhole. He looked at Drinkwater's coffin, now no more than a few feet away from him. The Teacher's had worn off, and all at once he felt incurably tired. It occurred to him that you could probably tell a joke whose punch line involved a choice between being dead and being outrighted to Buffalo. It didn't seem like much of a choice, but he supposed that Buffalo held a slight edge. On the other hand, at least Drinkwater didn't have to know that he had died.

He had the vague impression that something was disturbing his exhaustion and then realized that it was Coleman Drinkwater, pulling on his sleeve. The little boy pointed at the coffin. He was watching it as though he had been told that it was going to perform a trick.

"Is my daddy in there?" he said, in a clear, thin, terribly normal voice.

Magee and Coleman looked at each other for what became several seconds. Magee, who had no children, searched for the correct way to answer. He wanted to say something that would be fair to Coleman and yet would not make him afraid. He wished that his head were clearer and that he were not so damn tired. He felt as though everyone in the church were waiting on his reply. His forehead grew damp and he opened his mouth, but he said nothing. Finally, helpless, he put an arm around Coleman's small shoulders, and turned back to the speaker in the pulpit. The little boy suffered his godfather's arm upon him, and as the funeral dragged on he even rested his head against Magee's rib cage. Presently he fell asleep.

After a while, Magee himself, who had been awake for some thirty-two hours, drifted into an easy sleep. He dreamed his usual dream, the one in which he had found his stuff again and was on the mound at Three Rivers throwing seven different kinds of smoke. The sunshine was fragrant and the grass brilliant. When he awoke, feeling refreshed, the funeral was over and the coffin had already been wheeled out. Beryl was standing in front of him, her arms folded, looking as she had once looked on bailing him out of the Erie County Prison. Magee smiled, rubbed his eyes, and then realized that Coleman and Roxille had gone. He spun around in time to see the little boy being towed by his mother out the front door of the church. Coleman smiled across the empty pews at Magee, who saw from this distance that the design shaved into the side of the little boy's head was not two eyeballs. It was Eli Drinkwater's uniform number, the double zero.

"Poor kid," said Beryl. "I heard what he asked you. God. I almost lost it."

"I know," said Magee, scratching his chin. He could not seem to remember what his reply had been, or if he had said anything at all.

"So," said Beryl, sitting down beside him and taking hold of his throwing hand. She began, with a firm, nursely touch, to massage it. The backs of her hands hadn't aged very much at all, and Magee, feeling nostalgic, watched them for a while as they worked him over. A soft lock of her platinum hair brushed against his cheek. "So. What are you going to do? Buffalo? You're really going to let them do that to you?"

"I want to pitch, Ber. I have to get my mechanics back. I think it'll be a little easier in Triple A."

Beryl tightened her grasp on his hand and looked at him. Her face was neither incredulous nor mocking; she only bit her lip and wrinkled the bridge of her nose. Beryl's nose, though small, could be expressive of great sadness.

"Magee," she said. "Matty. Maybe I'm wrong to even put this thought in your head. I know how hard you're trying, Matty, but—what if they're just gone, baby?" Her voice cracked sweetly as she said this. "Have you ever thought of that?"

Magee withdrew his pitching hand and flexed it a couple of times. He watched it with a puzzled expression, as though it were a new model, of uncertain capacity. Then he looked away from it, up toward the ceiling of the church, and tried, for the last time, to remember if he had answered Coleman Drinkwater, and what he had told him.

"Yes," he said to the empty choir.

MILLIONAIRES

At one time Harry and I shared everything; it is an error common to fast friendship. We idolized the same artists, movies, and ballplayers (particularly Cornell, *The Conversation,* and Madlock) and liked our food—even our breakfasts—with equally generous garnishes of the Vietnamese hot sauce we purchased at Tran's on Murray Avenue. We wore each other's clothes and merged our record collections. The expenses on our apartment and the grocery bills we paid with one another's money, spending in a rough and free rotation until both of us were broke. The one thing we were unable to share—of course—was female companionship. When Harry began to sleep with Ruthie Louise Dollar or Atalanta Chin, or I with Evelyn Smrek, we did our best to stay above it, and made nervous jokes about the young woman and about the beast with three backs, but a shadow would fall across our friendship for the duration of the affair.

Nevertheless, Harry and I were still living together after the advents and ascensions of a good dozen girlfriends, and there was a special shelf above the radiator in the bathroom on which we displayed a tortoiseshell barrette, a gold Star of David on a chain, and a plaster impression of Ruthie Louise's snaggled lower teeth, made by her orthodontist when she was in junior high, which had somehow come into Harry's possession. I regret to say that in conversation we took a good deal of pride in our friendship's proven invulnerability to women; and I kept to myself the potentially disruptive information that I was in love with his newest girlfriend, Kim Trilby, and that there were many Saturday nights during the winter they were together upon which, as I lay alone and shivering on my futon in the empty house, the thought of Harry and Kim sleeping spoonwise and naked in Kim's hot bedroom made me wish that he were dead.

I was working at the time as a disk jockey for a failing A.O.R. station that not long afterward went all-polka and cornered a small but solid share of the market. There was a high-watt, long-established rock-and-roll station two point six notches to the right, and no one listened to WDAN except, I imagined, people in hotel rooms who chose it on their clock radio for their wakeup call on the morning they left Pittsburgh forever. I had a Sunday-to-Friday midnight-to-six slot that wrecked my social life but afforded me the opportunity to talk a lot of outrageous nonsense in a variety of voices and now and then slip in a cut by Blurt or the Virgin Prunes without fear that anyone might hear it and complain. On the air I became once more an only child in his room on a rainy Saturday afternoon with his dolls and his record player, temporarily unaware of the weight of loneliness upon me.

Very early one Tuesday morning in March—I remember

it was still dark, and there were three nurses waiting for a bus on the corner—I came in from the bone-snapping cold to find several lights on and the apartment warm. It surprised me to find Harry home, and awake, since lately he had taken to spending almost every night at Kim's, over on Beacon, but I was even more surprised that he had turned on the steam heat. Out of Harry's chronic tightfistedness—we were responsible for half of the heating bill—and some perverse impulse of mine to test our seven years' friendship, we had at some point during December made a tacit pact never to open the radiators, and ever since had been going around the house in our ski caps and down coats, exhaling puffs of vapor in the frigid bathroom and wearing gloves to cook dinner; the clouds of steam produced by the act of dumping a boiling pot of spaghetti into a colander in the sink were thick and billowing. It was a kind of dare, to see who would succumb first to the cold, but it did not please me to discover that I had won. Something was the matter with Harry.

"Hey!" I said, walking through the empty living room—we had one chair. I imagined that Harry would be in the kitchen, fixing breakfast, but there was no reply. I let my coat and scarf fall to the floor around me, listening for his footsteps or his voice talking on the telephone. Just as I was about to call his name again, there was the sound of a breaking dish or glass from the basement. We were on the first floor of a two-story house that had been made into a duplex, and the way to the basement was through our apartment. There was another explosion of glass, then another, then several more in rapid succession, as though Harry had set a row of tumblers along the top of the washing machine and were now blowing them off with an air rifle. He did not own an air rifle, however, and I ran, almost falling, down the steps, knowing that at their base I would find my friend heartbroken and half in the bag.

In fact, I found him in just his boxer shorts and ski cap, holding a half-empty bottle of George Dickel in his right hand and one of my late mother's Franciscan dinner plates in his left. His left arm was raised and cocked at the elbow, and he held the plate as for a flea-flicker into the end zone. The service for twelve was part of my mother's legacy to me and she had intended me to present it to whatever unfortunate woman might become my bride. On the concrete floor all about him lay one hundred and twenty-seven shards of consolation. I knew at once that he'd split up with Kim; I had seen him in the mood to shatter things many times before. As usual he wore a smile, peculiar to this mood, that combined the glee of the vandal with the grim, self-loathing amusement of the drunk. The ski cap was pulled down crookedly over one eye, and this, when he whirled toward me and brandished the plate and the bottle of whiskey, gave him a piratical air. He was a big fellow, wore a full black beard, and his left eye, I saw, had been badly blackened.

"Well, she's all yours, Vince!" he said, in an ugly voice.

"It's my bedtime," I said, suddenly very tired. "Why are you doing this now?"

Harry was always considerate of my hours—he suffered from intermittent insomnia, and held sleep in high esteem—and he set the dish down on the floor with a drunken gentleness.

"I'm sorry," he said. "I guess Kim dumped me."

"You guess?"

"It's one of those."

"You mean you might have dumped her."

"It's possible."

"Did she give you that shiner?" Not too long before this, Kim and a baseball bat had broken up a knife fight at the bar where she worked, the Squirrel Cage—maybe you saw that jerk Snake Fleming walking around with his head all bandaged—and she had a reputation, despite her size, for being pretty good with her fists.

"What shiner?" said Harry. He took a long swallow from the bottle of Dickel. It went down a little rough, and this seemed to sober him up for a minute. He looked around him at the wreckage of my mother's dishes and frowned.

"It was the toys," he said at last.

Harry was the director of research and development for Other Worlds, Inc., a Pittsburgh firm that manufactured what its advertisements called "playthings for the unusual child," or, as Harry described them, "toys for kids nobody will like in high school." It was a small firm, and Harry constituted the entire department. The president and other half of the firm was an elderly Orthodox man named Mr. Levinsky, a thirties socialist and tri-state sales representative for Platt & Munk, or Funk & Wagnalls—I forget which—who now devoted his days to driving all over the eastern seaboard attending customs auctions and buying up abandoned shipments of whatever looked interesting and cheap. All manner of odd and useless items, in huge lots, are auctioned off every day in the ports of the East: twelve hundred hydraulic fan blades, nine thousand spools of orange thread, fifty-two cases of baby-food jars, a half-mile of plastic forks still on their sprues. Mr. Levinsky and Claude, the company driver, would return with these prizes, in a drug-bust–impounded Mercedes truck that Mr. Levinsky had also bought at auction, to the Other Worlds warehouse, in Monroeville.

It was Harry's job to attempt to play with each item, to discover if it had any "intrinsic ludic value," as Mr. Levinsky put it, apart from its intended function. Harry would devise some way of building with it, or decorating his body, or annoying his elders, and then the item would be packed in an attractive box and sold nationally for $24.95 at museum gift shops and at toy stores with track lighting and Scandinavian-sounding names. Harry's greatest success so far had been Odd Ject. You've seen it—an assortment of polystyrene balls, golf tees, and those multicolored cocktail toothpicks that have a lock of curly cellophane hair at one end. This "Self-Generating Deconstruction Kit" had caught on the Christmas before, selling out eighteen thousand units in two and a half weeks, and had earned him a raise and a rare handshake from Mr. Levinsky. The chief drawback of his otherwise enviable line of work was that it led Harry to regard every object around him—his shoes, a box of brads, a woman's birth-control-pill dispenser—as a potential plaything. In the middle of

a serious conversation about the Supreme Court or chla-
mydia, you would catch him poking straightened paper clips
into a sponge, staging a mock naval battle with dry mac-
aroni, or rolling his pocket lint into the shapes of animals
and setting them on parade. I mention the pill dispenser
because this was the item that had precipitated his break
with Kim.

"They make really cool spaceships," said Harry. He
sagged to his knees and began to sweep up the broken dishes
with his hands. "When you turn the dial, you can pop the
pills out like little, uh, hormone bombs. Pow. Pow. An
entire population suddenly unable to conceive."

"Harry," I said. "Come on upstairs. I'm going to bed
now."

"There's this way you can make them shoot really far."

"Leave the mess. Come on."

I took him by the arm, guided him to the steps, and
gave him a little push. He returned the push, more forcefully, and I fell backward. My head cracked against the floor
and I heard within my skull the sound of a rock hitting a
sheet of taut aluminum. I smelled blood in my nose and I
imagined, for a half second, that I was about to pass away.
I lived.

"Stay away from her," he said. "I know what you have
in mind."

It was a while before I was able to speak. "You asshole,"
I said. "I don't have anything in mind."

This was not, I realized as I said it, entirely true. I had
already begun to form vague plans to unbutton Kim's blouse,

remove her cowboy boots, peel off her blue jeans, and lick her body from sole to crown. The pain in my head was all at once as nothing.

"Oh, my God, you're bleeding, Vince," said Harry. He extended a hand and then pulled me to my feet. I touched a finger to my nose and smiled at him.

"You just made a big mistake," I said.

I awoke early that afternoon, showered, and performed my toilet with the care of a man intent on seduction. Kim worked as a waitress at the Squirrel Cage and did not go on until evening, and I expected to find her at home. I had come to believe in my interchangeability with Harry so completely that it did not occur to me that Kim would have any qualms about going to bed with a new partner while still in the midst of a painful breakup; I simply assumed that she would have me, as she would have had Harry, as though he'd called in sick and I were the equally qualified temporary sent by some Kelly Services of love. I had known her as long as he had, and we got along well. She was a thin, raspy-voiced woman with a sarcastic manner, expressive hands, and a respectable knowledge of what is sometimes known as industrial rock—a particular favorite of mine. I had taken her once to see my friend Lee Skirboll perform in a band called Hex Wrench, for which Lee beat on a steel filing cabinet with an assortment of golf clubs and spatulas while his partner sat in on tape deck, amplified shortwave radio, and a bank of old-fashioned Philco sine-wave generators supplied, without his knowing it, by Mr. Levinsky. Kim had enjoyed it, and, I now reminded myself, lathering my chin with increasing zeal, there had been a furtive kiss and hand squeeze in the instant before we'd gone into the bar, where we were rendezvousing with Harry, who liked only Debussy, De Falla, and Erik Satie.

When I came out to the dining table—the heat was turned off again, and I wore my gloves and a hat—there was a note from Harry propped against the sugar bowl. "SORRY," it read. "JESUS, WHAT A HEADACHE I HAVE. YOU MUST TOO. SORRY SORRY SORRY. H." As a matter of fact, I had a rather large lump on the back of my head, and a faint sensation of pain if I turned too quickly; otherwise I was all right. Beside the note were looped five dozen yards of very thin telephone wire, in seven colors with contrasting stripes, that Harry had been experimenting with recently for his long-planned masterpiece, Aporia—an "inverted board game" whose rules changed unpredictably with each roll of the dice but whose outcome was always the same. I sat down with a cup of coffee and idly picked up a length of yellow-and-blue wire. I had grown up in a young community in which there was a continual construction of houses all through my youth, and I remembered finding this kind of wire at the building sites and twisting it into finger rings, single loops of wire—about that wide for Kim's finger, I guessed—along which you wrapped little coils, like this, pressed together so that in the end each coil made a bead, yellow or blue. After ten minutes' work I had a handsome piece, the sight of which recalled to me a hopeful love offering of my boyhood that had not been rejected. I slipped it into my pocket and went, almost skipping, out the front door.

It was much warmer outside than inside, and I soon shed my hat and gloves and stuffed them into the pocket of my coat. The sun shone most promisingly, there was a slight gasoline hint of summer traffic in the air, and on the lawn of the Methodist church on the corner I saw blades of early daffodils where a few days before there had been a crust of old snow. A warm breeze blew up along the sidewalk, and it seemed to me I had only to kick twice and thrust upward my chin in order to lift off the pavement and glide, touching down every twenty feet or so, toward the house of my slender love. People in cars had their windows rolled down, and I could hear the airy music from their radios as they passed. Now I unzipped my coat and rocked my head from side to side. The resultant ache was poignant and appropriate. Two elderly men emerged from Isaly's, both of them biting into the first Klondikes of the season, and I sailed after them along Murray Avenue, listening as they argued about the potential of a good-hitting shortstop the Pirates had decided to promote from the minors. Oh, I thought, it is almost Opening Day!

When I arrived at Kim's door I found to my surprise that I had lost the better part of my desire to sleep with her. It would be nice to see her, to sit down in her sunny kitchen and look at some absurd daytime program on the television—we had done that many times before—but I was so happy just then, slapping up the concrete steps with my coat flapping behind me and the warmth of my body rising up through my open collar in a fragrant column of air, that I didn't think anything, not even taking her into my arms, could improve my mood. The sexual act, in prospect, seemed to offer only danger and regret.

I proceeded more cautiously up the three steps of her front porch and across to her front door, and as soon as I rang her doorbell I wished that I had not. I wavered a moment on the welcome mat, then fled back down the steps; but there was no time to get away without being seen. I looked this way, then that, turned back toward the door, turned away. I heard her tread in the hallway, her hand on the knob, and at the last possible moment I ducked between the concrete skirt of the porch and the low hedge of holly that concealed it, crouching in the dirt, in the narrow space between the prickling holly and the house. A thorn scratched my cheek as she opened the door, and it was all I could do to keep from cursing.

There was a long pause during which I had time to realize that I was crouching in a hard pile of snow and my butt was getting very wet. I heard Kim sniffle a few times, as though she were smelling me out, and then a beleaguered sigh.

"You have hat-head, Vince," she said. "As usual."

I rose, pulled the hat from my pocket, and put it back on my head. It might have been the hat—perhaps it was enchanted—or simply the sight of Kim in a long cable sweater that sagged at the neck and reached down to the tops of her knees; in any case, as soon as I saw her I wanted her again. Harry was my best friend, but millionaires have squandered their fortunes, and men have lost their minds, and friends have tracked each other down for less than the sight of a lovely woman in nothing but a sweater.

"I slept in my hat," I said. "As usual. Don't ever let

your life get to the point where you have to sleep with your hat on."

"Come on in. It's nice and warm."·

"I know it is."

I followed her into the house and down her long front hallway to the kitchen, where the radio played and there was a smell of bay leaf, onion, and fresh dirt.

"I'm making lentil soup," she said, turning to the stove and peering into a cast-iron pot. In the bulky sweater Kim looked plump and wifely; she who was so thin that Harry would sometimes clean and jerk her over his head and spin around calling, "Choppers! Incoming wounded!" At the time she couldn't have weighed more than ninety-five pounds. "This'll be the last lentil soup of the winter, I guess."

"Looks like it."

"You can have some when it's ready."

"Thanks."

"If you promise not to mention Harry."

"I can promise that," I said.

The old pink radio on the kitchen table emitted a familiar promo. Two bars of the psycho-kazoo opening to "Crosstown Traffic," followed by the synthesized effect of a starship's landing, and then my own voice, filtered and phased, sounding as though I were a twenty-seven–foot black man about to get very angry. "WDAN!" said my disturbing voice. "Huge Music!"

"*You're* the one who listens," I said. In general I pretended that it did not trouble me to labor in the ratings cellar, but at the discovery that Kim tuned in to that doomed little station, I was moved and took it as incontestable proof of her rightness for me.

"Harry makes me," she said.

She carefully straddled a kitchen chair and motioned for me to do the same. I sat. I looked at the ashtray between us, in which there were fifteen or sixteen bent butts. Kim smoked far too much, even for a waitress. Now she lit another.

"I'm going to have to stop," she said, in a sad little voice, as though it had never occurred to her before.

"Sure you are."

"You'll see," she said. "Was he trashed when you got home?"

"Oh, no, not really," I said.

"Don't lie."

"He was breaking my mother's dishes in the basement."

"Oh, boy."

"And he had the heat on."

She put down her cigarette, and her brown eyes got very wide and surprised.

Then she laughed, without sarcasm, with a happiness so genuine that I was taken aback. It was deep and caroling laughter, and it seemed to invite me to turn Harry, the idea of Harry, into a risible fool, to flatten him into a cartoon character and laugh him right out of her affections. This was the simple task before me.

"What's so funny?" I said; the question sounded more harsh than I had intended.

"Nothing," said Kim. She looked down at the coal of her cigarette and bit her lip.

"Kimberly Ellen Donna Marie Trilby," I said. I went over to her chair and knelt on the floor beside her. She sat, looking at her cigarette and calmly crying. I didn't know why she was crying, whether because Harry was gone or because I was still there, but I felt very sorry for her. Once in a while you will see a waitress like that, crying at the back of a restaurant or in the hallway by the phone, staring down at a monogrammed matchbook in her fingers, and consider for a second or two the untold hardness of a waitress's life. I reached around and pulled her to me. There followed the briefest of struggles before she fell sprawling into my arms.

"Come with me," she said, after a minute or two. She stood and led me down the hallway and into her bedroom. Her gait was too brisk to be seductive; she had some business to attend to. I had been in her bedroom many times before, had felt the thrill of seeing her white bedclothes and rows of empty shoes, but never with this acute a sense of being suffered, like a smelly old dog on a miserable night, just this once allowed to sleep indoors, on the still warm hearth—of being such a lucky dog.

On her bed there stood a large cardboard Seagram's box, taped shut, and bearing, in Harry's antic handwriting, the Magic Markered label TREASURE.

"What's in the box?" I said.

"I have no idea." She looked at it as though it might go off any second. "He brought it over yesterday after work. Will you give it back to him for me?"

"He didn't say what was in it?"

"I didn't ask. I stopped asking questions about his junk a long time ago."

"Because you didn't love him anymore," I said, taking hold of her chin and drawing her to my lips. At this mild demonstration of amorous force—an effect I have never been adept at pulling off—she put her knee into my stomach, firmly, and I fell gasping to the floor.

"I will always love Harry," said Kim. "I will always, always love Harry."

"I understand that," I said.

"I'm sorry I kicked you."

"Thanks," I said, getting up. "I'm sorry, too. It was just all that kissing we did back there in the kitchen."

"Sure it was."

"Wait here," I said. I sighed, as much to catch my breath as to register my impatience with her and with Harry's goddam toys, then picked up the cardboard box and carried it out of the room.

"I know what to do with it," I called over my shoulder.

"What?" she said, with a strange furrow in her voice. She followed me out of the door and laid a restraining hand on my shoulder. "What are you going to do with it? Vince?"

"You'll see."

The box was a good deal heavier than it looked, and I wondered, as I bore it out of the kitchen door and down the back steps, what might be in it, and why Harry had packed it all up in this way and left it sitting on Kim Trilby's bed. The sun was still shining, there in the backyard amid the skinny poplars and the rusted-out Kelvinator with its door chained shut, and it was going to be a beautiful afternoon. I set the treasure down on the brittle grass and went into the cellar, where I had left the battered old spade I'd used to shovel the walk all that winter, ostensibly for the benefit of Kim's upstairs landlady, Mrs. Colodny, who afterward would always feed me frozen kishkes from the KosherMart. The spade in question had got hidden, I saw, behind a stack of Harry's boxes marked BEEHIVE PANELS and G.I. JOE HEADS in the far corner, but I got it out and went straight to work.

"Come on, Vince," said Kim, calling to me from the back steps of her apartment. "That's Mrs. Colodny's dirt you're messing up. Hey, Vince, come on. I get it, O.K.?"

I grinned at her and kept on. Digging is one of the most difficult of boring chores, if I have not transposed the adjectives, and it took me a good fifteen minutes of sweating and cursing, but when I finished I was wet and hot and exhilarated and the thing was three feet under the ground. Kim stayed where she was, hugging herself in that loose sweater and lighting a third cigarette with her second. I leaned on the spade, and for a moment we regarded one another across the lawn. I didn't know what I had proved, exactly, and she probably didn't know what had impressed her, but I had proved something, and she looked impressed. I let the spade fall, went to her, and rested my head against the doorjamb, breathing hard, and waited for Kim to throw herself, without regret, without apprehension, into my faithless embrace.

"What happens to it now?" she said, staring bitterly out

into the sunny backyard at the black patch of earth I had uncovered.

"I don't know," I said. "I guess that would depend on what it is." Perhaps, I speculated guiltily, Harry had packed up every note I'd ever left him, and all of the baseball cards and *Playboys* I had bought him when his asthma got bad, and the cigar box of ancient Inuit teeth from my trip to Alaska that he'd said he needed, and the French edition of *Tropic of Cancer* labeled, thrillingly, "Not to be taken into the U.S.A.," which I'd picked up for him at the Bryn Mawr-Vassar bookstore on Winthrop Street one day. There might have been some pretty swell stuff in that box; I realized that.

"You don't know," she said. "I like that." She grinned, as though she could be satisfied with this response, at least for an hour or two.

Early that evening, in her bedroom, she awoke with a start. She was trembling, and she felt so frail that I was afraid I had harmed her somehow in our thrashings and busculation, and when she lit a cigarette it frightened me to hear the rattle in her breast as she exhaled—a terrible sound like the shivering of withered leaves on a branch.

"Put out that cigarette and come on back to bed," I cried.

"All right," she said, with an odd tenderness. As she slid down under the covers again, I leaned over, found my trousers in the heap of clothes on the floor, and reached into the left pocket. My fingers closed around the wire ring and held it fast. I was afraid that we had made a profound, irrevocable mistake, and that, as in a fantastic tale, if I did not find something firm and magical to grab hold of right that moment we would both be swallowed up by a noisome gang of black shapes and evil black birds. We made a tent of the bedclothes with our knees, and sat within this intimate yurt, breathing one another's exhalations and listening to everything around us. After a moment, as the air grew thick and sweet, I found her left hand, counted off the fingers, and then slipped on the ring. (It was a little too big, but it would come, eventually, to fit her.) I lifted it, with her fingers, to my mouth, and printed a kiss upon them. Our tent collapsed and the cold March evening, with its last gray skies, flooded in. I was panting with relief. I would figure out something to tell Harry, both about Kim and about the thing I had buried, and we would all just have to adjust.

"I have to get to work," said Kim, twisting the ring around on her finger as though it chafed her, or as though to invoke whatever doubtful protection its loops of wire might provide. Then she turned to me, smiling, and said something hopeful about the baby she was going to bear, and I smiled back at her in the dimness, as though I had known about it all along. I did not admit—as I ought to have, God knows—that the bauble I had given her was really only a toy.

I dropped in on Harry not too long ago. These days he shares a four-room flat in East Liberty with two Japanese girls named Tomoko. We're still friends, I guess—to the extent that we can make each other laugh—but it's rare that we get together for longer than a few hours, and our relations have passed into that stage at which they draw their greatest animation from beer and reminiscence. Usually when I see him, at Chief's or at the Electric Banana, there is a third person present—some friend of his whom I don't get along with, or a woman I work with whom Harry dislikes—and our conversation is ungainly, unfamiliar, and touches not upon important matters.

Since the day Kim left us, we have never truly talked about her—I doubt if we will ever be able to talk seriously about Kim again—nor have we succeeded in forgetting her and putting all that behind us. For one thing, there are the pictures of little Raymond James Trilby that Kim sends both Harry and me from time to time. Then there is the odd evening when Harry and I run into each other at the Squirrel Cage, where, in a frame over the bar, right next to the sign that reads IT'S NICE TO BE IMPORTANT BUT IT'S MORE IMPORTANT TO BE NICE, you will still find a carnival-midway caricature of Kim brandishing a Louisville Slugger. And another constant reminder, I guess you could say, is the large, whistling hole that was torn in the fabric of our lives by my marriage to and then divorce from Kim—a hole that opens onto frigid emptiness and the brilliant debris of stars. We were married for seven months in all, and toward the end Kim was—almost despite herself—eating her dinner more often with Harry than with me, and calling him constantly to bitch and commiserate. And then one day, a family of purple lint polar bears appeared on top of the clothes dryer, amid the flakes of Ivory Snow, and in the kitchen wastebasket we found a crumpled squadron of cigarette-foil fighter jets; and Kim, who had already made one or two mistakes, got out of Pittsburgh as quickly as she could.

When I stopped by Harry's the other night, the two Tomokos were out for the evening with a visitor from Nagoya, and after Harry had shown me their neat beds, their pastel closets, the photos on their walls, and samples of their handwriting, and had generally filled me in on them and on his own xenophilia, we sat down in the living room, on opposite sides of a six-pack of Rolling Rock, and looked at each other. I am not seeing anyone at present and had few accounts to amuse him with in this regard.

"So it sounds like you've been very busy," I said.

"Really busy," he said. "How about you?"

"Busy."

There ensued an awkward pause, during which I might easily have drained my beer, slapped my knee, and slipped off into the October evening—the sun had gone down distressingly early. I could not think of anything to say, not a single thing, and I saw how much I had come to depend on the presence of a third person at our meetings—on having someone there to fill up the awful gap in our facetious conversation. I looked again at Harry's beard, which had of late grown to mermanish proportions, floating out from his face. Then I looked all around me. "It's nice and warm in here," I said at last.

"Oh, my God," he said, shivering in recollection. "I can't believe we lived that way. Do you remember that one morning there was a, like, a skin of ice on the water in the toilet?"

"Oh, God, I remember," I said.

"Ha."

"Hmm."

"Have you heard anything from Kim?" he said, standing, making for the refrigerator to cover the question. I said that I had not, nor had I any news of little Raymond James. I understood from Kim's mother, whom I'd met in the Giant Eagle a couple of months before, that Kim was working out of Honolulu as a personal secretary on board a rich woman's yacht, but someone else had told me she was working as a paralegal in Philadelphia. Harry said he had heard these reports already and disbelieved them both. He handed me another can of beer.

"Funny how that all ended up, huh?" he said.

"Funny."

"I pretty much bailed on her, I guess. On the baby, too."

We sipped our beers and wondered at one another, at what was left of all that and of those prodigal days.

"Not too funny, really," Harry said.

"Kind of not too funny at all," I said.

The telephone rang, and Harry went into the kitchen to answer it. He spoke in curt and secretive tones to some friend I would never meet, promising—ah, but this came as a blow to me—that he would be free to call him or her back in a little while. He returned with a mostly empty bottle of George Dickel and a long face.

"Maybe I'd better go, Harry," I said.

"Oh, no!" he said, looking so earnest that my doubts were almost erased. "I have things to show you."

He took me down into the basement of the house, where there were a washer and dryer, three bicycles, a stranded toilet lying on its side, some camping gear—including two voided backpacks bearing Rising Suns and some of those horrific Hello Kitty patches—and a vast assortment of cardboard cartons, perhaps sixty or seventy in all, stacked in ragged stacks and labeled in Harry's familiar, Mayan-looking handwriting: PIPE TAMPERS, VELVETEEN, HEMP, SQUARE BUTTONS, GUM ARABIC, MR. POTATO HEAD HATS, ATOMIZER BULBS, PLASTIC SUSHI REPLICAS, FAN BELTS, LITTLE RED MONKEYS. He showed me the plans for a new game called Car Crash, involving bottle caps, miniature Christmas light bulbs, tin-whistle sirens, and cans of some knockoff red Play-Doh from Malaysia, and then, crouching down on the floor and reaching in behind the carton of gum arabic, drew out a large square box.

"This is going to be my next toy," he said. "I'm calling it Treasure."

This time the word TREASURE was machine-stenciled on the box's sides, in large letters, along with the name of a leading British toy manufacturer and the two words "Spanish Main," in Old English type.

"They tried to market it over here, but it stiffed early," he explained, opening the seal on the box with his thumbnail. "Levinsky made a killing in Baltimore on a misdelivered shipment of game pieces."

I watched his face for any sign that he was toying with me, but there was none; he seemed to want only to show me, with a hint of desperation, what was inside the crate, as though the hardest part of it for him had been having no one in whom to confide the secrets of his fabulous vault. He lifted the flaps to reveal a king's ransom, a cool million, in cardboard doubloons, painted gold and dimly glittering in the basement light, and I wondered if this was what had been in the box I'd buried in Mrs. Colodny's yard, or if it had been some other treasure entirely. I knew little about the subject, but I hoped that once you had buried a treasure you did not have to keep reburying it again and again.

"It's supposedly real gold dust in the paint," Harry said. "That was the gimmick, I guess."

He handed me a thick coin, and I examined it. It bore an illegible mock inscription and a crude cartoon of an emperor's head, and as I fingered it some of its luster came away on my hands. Harry was looking right at me now with a fevered smile, and once more I didn't know what to say, but there was no one else there, and I had to say something.

"We're rich," I said.

PART II

THE LOST WORLD

THE
LITTLE KNIFE

One Saturday in that last, interminable summer before his parents separated and the Washington Senators baseball team was expunged forever from the face of the earth, the Shapiros went to Nags Head, North Carolina, where Nathan, without planning to, perpetrated a great hoax. They drove down I-95, through the Commonwealth of Virginia, to a place called the Sandpiper—a ragged, charming oval of motel cottages painted white and green as the Atlantic, and managed by a kind, astonishingly fat old man named Colonel Larue, who smoked cherry cigars and would, if asked, play catch or keep-away. Outside his office, in the weedy gravel, stood an old red-and-radium-white Coke machine, which dispensed bottles from a vertical glass door that sighed when you opened it, and which reminded Nathan of the Automat his grandmother had taken him to once in New York City. The sight of the faded machine and of the whole Sandpiper—like that of the Automat—filled Nathan with a happy sadness, or, really, a sad happiness; he was not too young, at ten, to have developed a sense of nostalgia.

There were children in every cottage—with all manner of floats, pails, paddles, trucks, and flying objects—and his younger brother Ricky, to Nathan's envy, immediately fell in with a gang of piratical little boys with water pistols, who were always reproducing fart sounds and giggling chaotically when their mothers employed certain ordinary words such as "hot dog" and "rubber." The Shapiros went to the ocean every summer, and at the beginning of this trip, as on all those that had preceded it, Nathan and his brother got along better than they usually did, their mother broke out almost immediately in a feathery red heat rash, and their father lay pale and motionless in the sun, like a monument, and always forgot to take off his wristwatch when he went into the sea. Nathan had brought a stack of James Bond books and his colored pencils; there were board games—he and his father were in the middle of their Strat-O-Matic baseball playoffs—and miniature boxes of cereal; the family ate out every single night. But when they were halfway through the slow, dazzling week—which was as far as they were to get—Nathan began to experience an unfamiliar longing: He wanted to go home.

He awoke very early on Wednesday morning, went into the cottage's small kitchen, where the floor was sticky and the table rocked and trembled, and chose the last of the desirable cereals from the Variety pack, leaving for Ricky only those papery, sour brands with the scientific names—the sort that their grandparents liked. As he began to eat, Nathan heard, from the big bedroom down the hall, the unmistakable, increasingly familiar sound of his father burying his mother under a heap of scorn and ridicule. It was, oddly, a soft and pleading sound. Lately, the conversation and actions of Dr. Shapiro's family seemed to disappoint him terribly. His left hand was always flying up to smack his sad and outraged forehead, so hard that Nathan often thought he could hear his father's wedding ring crack against his skull. When they'd played their baseball game the day before—Nathan's Baltimore Bonfires against his father's Brooklyn Eagles—every decision Nathan made led to a disaster, and his father pointed out each unwise substitution and foolish attempt to steal in this new tone of miserable sarcasm, so that Nathan had spent the afternoon apologizing, and, finally, crying. Now he listened for his mother's voice, for the note of chastened shame.

The bedroom door slammed, and Mrs. Shapiro came out into the kitchen. She was in her bathrobe, a wild, sleepless smile on her face.

"Good morning, honey," she said, then hummed to herself as she boiled water and made a cup of instant coffee. Her spoon tinkled gaily against the cup.

"Where are you going, Mom?" said Nathan. She had taken up her coffee and was heading for the sliding glass door that led out of the kitchen and down to the beach.

"See you, honey," she sang.

"Mom!" said Nathan. He stood up—afraid, absurdly, that she might be leaving for good, because she seemed so happy. After a few seconds he heard her whistling, and he went to the door and pressed his face against the wire screen. His mother had a Disney whistle, melodious and full, like a Scotsman's as he walks across a meadow in a brilliant kilt. She paced briskly along the ramshackle slat-and-wire fence, back and forth through the beach grass, drinking from the huge white mug of coffee and whistling heartily into the breeze; her red hair rose from her head and trailed like a defiant banner. He watched her observe the sunrise—it was going to be a perfect, breezy day—then continued to watch as she set her coffee on the ground, removed her bathrobe, and, in her bathing suit, began to engage in a long series of yoga exercises—a new fad of hers—as though she were playing statues all alone. Nathan was soon lost, with the fervor of a young scientist, in contemplation of his pretty, whistling mother rolling around on the ground.

"Oh, how can she?" said Dr. Shapiro.

"Yes," said Nathan, gravely, before he blushed and whirled around to find his father, in pajamas, staring out at Mrs. Shapiro. His smile was angry and clenched, but in his eyes was the same look of bleak surprise, of betrayal, that had been there when Nathan took out Johnny Sain, a slugging pitcher, and the pinch-hitter, Enos Slaughter, immediately went down on strikes. There were a hundred new things that interested Nathan's mother—bonsai, the Zuni, yoga, real estate—and although Dr. Shapiro had always been a liberal, generous, encouraging man (as Nathan had heard his mother say to a friend), and had at first happily helped her to purchase the necessary manuals, supplies, and coffee-table books, lately each new fad seemed to come as a blow to him—a going astray, a false step.

"How can she?" he said again, shaking his big bearded head.

"She says it's really good for you," said Nathan.

His father smiled down on his son ruefully, and tapped him once on the head. Then he turned and went to the refrigerator, hitching up his pajama bottoms. They were the ones patterned with a blue stripe and red chevrons—the ones that Nathan always imagined were the sort worn by the awkward, doomed elephant in the Groucho Marx joke.

Later that day, as they made egg-salad sandwiches to carry down to the beach, Dr. and Mrs. Shapiro fought bitterly, for the fifth time since their arrival. In the cottage's kitchen was a knife—a small, new, foreign knife, which Mrs. Shapiro admired. As she used it to slice neat little horseshoes of celery, she praised it again. "Such a good little knife," she said. "Why don't you just take it?" said Dr. Shapiro. The air in the kitchen was suddenly full of sharp, caramel smoke, and Dr. Shapiro ran to unplug the toaster.

"That would be stealing," said Nathan's mother, ignoring her husband's motions of alarm and the fact that their lunch was on fire. "We are not taking this knife, Martin."

"Give it to me." Dr. Shapiro held out his hand, palm up.

"I'm not going to let you—make me—dishonest anymore!" said his mother. She seemed to struggle, at first, not to finish the sentence she had begun, but in the end she turned, put her face right up to his, and cried out boldly. After her outburst, both adults turned to look, with a simultaneity that was almost funny, at their sons. Nathan hadn't the faintest notion of what his mother was talking about.

"Don't steal, Dad," Ricky said.

"I only wanted it to extract the piece of toast," said their father. He was looking at their mother again. "God damn it." He turned and went out of the kitchen.

Her knuckles white around the handle of the knife, their mother freed the toast and began scraping the burnt surfaces into the sink. Because their father had said "God damn," Ricky wiggled his eyebrows and smiled at Nathan. At the slamming of the bedroom door, Nathan clambered up suddenly from the rickety kitchen table as though he had found an insect crawling on his leg.

"Kill it!" said Ricky. "What is it?"

"What is it?" said his mother. She scanned Nathan's body quickly, one hand half raised to swat.

"Nothing," said Nathan. He took off his glasses. "I'm going for a walk."

When he got to the edge of the water, he turned to look toward the Sandpiper. At that time in Nags Head there were few hotels and no condominiums, and it seemed to Nathan that their little ring of cottages stood alone, like Stonehenge, in the middle of a giant wasteland. He set off down the beach, watching his feet print and following the script left in the sand by the birds for which the motel was named. He passed a sand castle, then a heart drawn with a stick enclosing the names Jimmy and Beth. Sometimes his heels sank deeply into the sand, and he noticed the odd marks this would leave—a pair of wide dimples. He discovered that he could walk entirely on his heels, and his trail became two lines of big periods. If he took short steps, it looked as though a creature—a bird with two peg legs—had come to fish along the shore.

He lurched a long way in this fashion, watching his feet, and nearly forgot his parents' quarrel. But when at last he grew bored with walking on his heels and turned to go back, he saw that his mother and father had also decided to take a walk, and that they were, in fact, coming toward him—clasping hands, letting go, clasping hands again. Nathan ran to meet them, and they parted to let him walk between them. They all continued down the beach, stooping to pick up shells, glass, dead crabs, twine, and all the colored or smelly things that Nathan had failed to take note of before. At first his parents exclaimed with him over these discoveries, and his father took each striped seashell into his hands, to keep it safe, until there were two dozen and they jingled there like money. But after a while they seemed to lose interest, and Nathan found himself walking a few feet ahead of them, stooping alone, glumly dusting his toes with sand as he tried to eavesdrop on their careless and incomprehensible conversation.

"Never again," his mother said at last.

Dr. Shapiro let the shells fall. He rubbed his hands together and then stared at them as though waking from a dream in which he had been holding a fortune in gold Straightening up so quickly that his head spun, Nathan let out a cry and pointed down at the sand beneath their feet, among the scattered shells. "Look at those weird tracks!" he cried.

They all looked down.

Speculation on the nature of the beast that went toeless down the shore went on for several minutes, and although Nathan was delighted at first, he soon began to feel embarrassed and, obscurely, frightened by the ease with which he had deceived his parents. His treachery was almost exposed when Ricky, carrying a long stick and wearing a riot of Magic Marker tattoos on his face and all down his arms, ran over to find out what was happening. The little boy immediately tipped back onto his heels, and would have taken a few steps like that had Nathan not grabbed him by the elbow and dragged him aside.

"Why do you have a dog on your face?" said Nathan.

"It's a jaguar," said Ricky.

Nathan bent to whisper into his brother's ear. "I'm tricking Mom and Dad," he said.

"Good," said Ricky.

"They think there's some kind of weird creature on the beach."

Ricky pushed Nathan away and then surveyed their mother and father, who were talking again, quietly, as though they were trying not to alarm their sons. "It can't be real," said Nathan's father.

Ricky's skin under the crude tattoos was tanned, his hair looked stiff and ragged from going unwashed and sea-tangled, and as he regarded their parents he held his skinny stick like a javelin at his side. "They're dumb," he said flatly.

Dr. Shapiro approached, stepping gingerly across the mysterious tracks, and then knelt beside his sons. His face was red, though not from the sun, and he seemed to have trouble looking directly at the boys. Nathan began to cry before his father even spoke.

"Boys," he said. He looked away, then back, and bit his lip. "I'm afraid—I'm sorry. We're going to go home. Your mom and I—don't feel very well. We don't seem to be well."

"No! No! It was Nathan!" said Ricky, laying down his spear and throwing himself into his father's arms. "It wasn't me. Make *him* go home."

Nathan, summoning up his courage, decided to admit that the curious trail of the crippled animal was his, and he said, "I'm responsible."

"Oh, no!" cried both his parents together, startling him. His mother rushed over and fell to her knees, and they took Nathan into their arms and said that it was never, never him, and they ruffled his hair with their fingers, as though he had done something they could love him for.

After they came back from dinner, the Shapiros, save Nathan, went down to the sea for a final, sad promenade. At the restaurant, Ricky had pleaded with his parents to stay through the end of the week—they had not even been to see the monument at Kitty Hawk, the Birthplace of Aviation. For Ricky's sake, Nathan had also tried to persuade them, but his heart wasn't in it—he himself wanted so badly to go home—and the four of them had all ended up crying and chewing their food in the brass-and-rope dining room of the Port O' Call; even Dr. Shapiro had shed a tear. They were going to leave that night. Nathan's family now stood, in sweatshirts, by the sliding glass door, his parents straining to adopt hard and impatient looks, and Nathan saw that they felt guilty about leaving him behind in the cottage.

"I'll pack my stuff," he said. "Just go." For a moment his stomach tightened with angry, secret glee as his mother and father, sighing, turned their backs on him and obeyed his small command. Then he was alone in the kitchen again, for the second time that day, and he wished that he had gone to look at the ocean, and he hated his parents, uncertainly, for leaving him behind. He got up and walked into the bedroom that he and Ricky had shared. There, in the twilight that fell in orange shafts through the open window, the tangle of their clothes and bedsheets, their scattered toys and books, the surfaces of the broken dresser and twin headboards seemed dusted with a film of radiant sand, as though the tide had washed across them and withdrawn, and the room was strewn with the seashells they had found. Nathan, after emptying his shoebox of baseball cards into his suitcase, went slowly around the room and harvested the shells with careful sweeps of his trembling hand. Bearing the shoebox back into the kitchen, he collected the few stray shards of salt-white and green beach glass that lay in a pile beside the electric can opener, and then added a hollow pink crab's leg in whose claw Ricky had fixed a colored pencil. When Nathan saw the little knife in the drainboard by the sink, he hesitated only a moment before dropping it into the box, where it swam, frozen, like a model shark in a museum diorama of life beneath the sea. Nathan chuckled. As clearly as if he were remembering them, he foresaw his mother's accusation, his father's enraged denial, and with an unhappy chuckle he foresaw, recalled, and fondly began to preserve all the discord for which, in his wildly preserving imagination, he was and would always be responsible.

MORE
THAN HUMAN

Throughout the dismal, inadequate spring that preceded his moving out of the house, Dr. Shapiro drew his sustenance and cheer from the evenings on which he and his son made library rounds. The Henrietta County Library System was wealthy and adventuring, and maintained well-provisioned outposts even at the farthest reaches of its empire, so that in only a few hours he and Nathan, like a bookish Mongol horde of two, could hit a dozen different libraries and return with a rich booty of fourteen-day New Arrivals and, for Nathan, books about baseball, mythology, and the exploits of civilized mice. Dr. Shapiro was trying to wean his son onto science fiction, according to the natural progression, as he had experienced it, from childhood to adolescence, and had been recommending the paranoid novels of his own youth—*Slan* and *The Demolished Man* and *What Mad Universe*—of which Nathan had preferred the first, whose youthful protagonist has two hearts.

There was avid competition for fourteen-day books in Henrietta County, which was the ostensible reason for these weekly raids and the explanation that Dr. Shapiro gave to his wife and even to Nathan. His true motive was his lifelong need of minor rituals, a need that had lately become almost compulsive as the extreme state of his marriage and the sadness of his new job—he was working at Sunny Valley Farms, a small private psychiatric clinic for children, where he was exposed to a great deal of various and fairly sinister childhood lunacy—had robbed his life of the quotidian and left him with all the surprising novelty of a nightmare. His pipe, his weekly move in his correspondence chess game, and his trips with Nathan across the backroads of Henrietta County were the only commonplace ceremonies he had.

On Thursday nights, when the libraries stayed open until nine, he would come home from work, shower, put on blue jeans and a clean shirt, and sit down to watch the last fifteen minutes of *Lost in Space* with Nathan. Dr. Shapiro, who at his son's age had attempted, according to a recipe given by an article in *Science Wonder Stories*, to create life in a laundry pail, took a guilty interest in the show, and had seen every absurd episode at least once. After it was over, he and Nathan would leave Rose and Ricky to their dinner, step, still chuckling, into the drizzle and hydrangea, and drive off. As he guided the car onto the winding old tobacco road that led across townhouse parks and cornfields to the Gunpowder Creek Branch, the unremarkable landscape and the quizzical conversation of his son would bore and relax him, and leave him feeling halfway blessed and less mindful of his grip on the wheel.

They made up nicknames for his colleagues at Sunny Valley and for Nathan's schoolmates, wrought long chains of bad puns, sang operatic versions of advertising jingles. Dr. Shapiro had few friends, and his older son, from the time of his first words, had been the chief partner in his imaginative life. He knew that it could not be good for a father to depend in this way on his child, and disapproved of himself for it; he supposed that his was not an adult need at all, and that he should long ago have surrendered the soothing foolishness of words. Once, he had been able to dwell with Nathan for hours on end in a perpetually expanding universe of nonsense, but as they both got older, and as marital unhappiness and financial ambition and the passage of time came increasingly to dominate his thoughts, these hours had shrunk to the three they spent visiting libraries each week. Dr. Shapiro's need had never diminished, however, and had, if anything, been strengthened, in recent months, by the changing character of their conversations. Nathan tended increasingly to pose difficult questions that required careful replies, asked him to explain the rings of Saturn, the partition of India, the New York subway. The ardor of Nathan's desire for facts seemed to quicken a sympathetic current within the father, and his heart would pound as he endeavored, despite damnable gaps in his knowledge, to provide his son with good information.

One Thursday evening, about two weeks before the beginning of the summer, Dr. Shapiro at last found himself faced with the task of explaining to Nathan the nature of divorce. He was loath to derange their weekly idyll with this particular collection of sad facts, but he had been putting it off for nearly a month now, and come Saturday he would—how incredible—no longer be living within the same building as his family. It would have to be tonight. It was a windy, damp evening with no trace of June in it, and as they drove into the pale, almost imperceptible sunset he toyed with the idea of leaving without saying a word, of truly deserting Nathan—as his own father had done, in a different way, a year ago. The thought of his own insubstantiality, of his capacity simply to vanish, was horrible and seductive.

They had just come from the G. Earl King Memorial Branch, sixth on their route, and were headed for Lucci's, the Italian delicatessen where they always broke their trip. Nathan, who'd been unusually silent all evening, had a stack of paperbacks balanced on the back of his bent right forearm and was attempting to play Quarters with them, to grasp them abruptly in his hand before they could fall. They kept spilling across the front seat, over and over, with a disturbed, truncated flutter, as of startled pigeons. One struck Dr. Shapiro on the cheek, and the boy jumped preemptively away so that his father could not strike back, but Dr. Shapiro did not respond. It seemed to him that the road flew beneath them, that they had not hit a single red light, that there was nothing to slow their hurtling career. They were less than five minutes from Lucci's. Generally, he knew, he burdened his son with bad news or disapprobation in restaurants, for reasons that were unclear to him, and he didn't want it to happen that way this time. Unless he spoke now, he would have to wait until after they had eaten their pink, oily submarines and were on their way to the Cross Fork Branch, the very best, when he would not want to spoil for Nathan the prospect of its luxurious Young Adults Room, with the potted palms and microfilm machines. He cleared his throat and cursed his own cowardice;

he foresaw himself stalling until the last possible moment, sputtering out the words in the darkness of their driveway as with a ponderous hand he restrained his son from getting out, as he cut the engine and the interior filled with the sighs and ticking of a car at journey's end.

"I'm sorry, Dad," said Nathan, arranging his books now into a neat and penitent stack on the seat between them and folding his hands in his lap.

"It's all right," Dr. Shapiro replied. Then he was aware of the throbbing of his cheek where the book had hit him, a triangular pain over the bone. "It was an accident."

"Yes, that's right," Nathan said. "It was an accident." The boy smiled at him with his wild teeth, and his bright eyes behind the heavy eyeglasses looked false, a little out of kilter, as though his son were a doll of humble workmanship. Like those of his patients, Nathan's was an almost heartbreakingly plain face, and in it he thought he could read the same short narrative of rage and confusion. He had resolved a hundred times not to be a doctor to his sons, not to listen for and study the messages coded in their sudden misbehaviors, and to allow his children to disarm and to perplex him, but as he looked at Nathan he saw quite clearly that the boy was cognizant, however dimly, of the fear and shame and failure his father could not bring himself to express, and had already begun—accidentally— to retaliate. Dr. Shapiro's information was suddenly an unbearable weight upon him, an iron belt around his chest.

"Ask me anything," he said, too loudly, taking his foot off the accelerator pedal. The car slowed and then drifted to a halt in the middle of Old Rolling Road, five hundred yards from the next intersection. "Isn't there anything you'd like me to explain?"

Nathan looked over his shoulder, out the rear window, then turned back to face Dr. Shapiro. He bit his lip and at the same time smiled the anxious, sober smile of someone confronted with the folly, the minor act of vandalism, of a friend on a drunken spree. The few drivers lined up behind them honked their horns, then swerved brusquely around, shaking their fists as though in encouragement. "Do it!" they exhorted him. "Let the kid have it!" For a moment they sat all alone in their car, in the empty roadway, as Nathan seemed to search for the name of some thing he didn't know or had until now never quite grasped.

"If I was a mutant," the boy said at last, his gaze falling on the gaudy cover of one of the paperbacks, a novel called *More Than Human*, "would you and Mom ever tell me?"

Dr. Shapiro gave a sigh that was like a laugh, weary and slight. "No," he said. He had turned his damp face toward the window, ashamed, unable to preserve his son any longer. "I think we would just have to let you find out for yourself." He braced himself for the sentence he was about to utter and pushed down on the gas. The car gathered speed and drew relentlessly toward the intersection. He opened his mouth to speak, closed it, opened it once more.

"Then I guess I already know," said Nathan, from whom he had failed to conceal, failed to deflect, failed to ward off all the hazardous radiations of adulthood, of knowledge, of failure itself.

* * *

On the day his father moved out, Nathan's parents sent him and Ricky to the mall with his friend Edward, a decision of which, on the whole, Nathan approved. Although a part of him was curious simply to see what it looked like when one's father carried his things, his books and records and pipes, out the door—he loved those rare occasions when Dr. Shapiro, puffing out his bearded cheeks, engaged in some heavy labor—he had caught a glimpse that morning of a liquor box, full of hats, on the floor of his parents' bedroom, and the sight of a black Russian hat made of fur that was swirled like a brain, which Nathan remembered his father wearing on some black-and-white winter day before Ricky was ever born, had filled him with such longing and anger that he was glad to spend the afternoon eating pizza and wishing for toys in the Huxley Mall, whose air was sweet with candles and soap, and bitter with the chlorine from the fountains.

By the time they got home their father had already gone. Mrs. Shapiro sat alone at the kitchen table. As the boys came in, she stood quickly and, before she hugged them, swept two coffee cups and a plate of crumbs off the table and into the sink, blushing strangely. In their mother's wet embrace Nathan felt all at once smothered, blind, panicked, as he sometimes did when play required that he climb into a refrigerator carton or a crawl space. He squirmed wildly out of her arms and drew back.

"If you two are just going to cry all day," he announced, "I don't want to be around." He felt very wicked as he said this, and retreated from the kitchen in confusion. He climbed the stairs to his bedroom but was drawn inexorably to his parents' door. It was ajar and he pushed at it with the tip of his big toe, as though he might startle some animal asleep on the bed. There were indentations in the carpet, he saw, from his father's dresser, his desk, his creaking armoire, a pattern of twelve little circles like the spots on a domino. It hadn't occurred to Nathan that Dr. Shapiro would take the furniture, and its absence, curiously, made him feel sorry for his father, who was going to have to make do with so little now. Would there be a bed in this unimaginable apartment? Would there be a soft leather chair that reclined?

He stood in the middle of the half-empty room for a minute or so, until his glance fell on a wastebasket that stood beside the space where his father's desk had been. It was mostly full of shirt cardboard and the white wrappers of coat hangers, but at the bottom he spied a crumpled yellow ball of legal paper, which he fished out and spread flat on the floor. It was some kind of a list, made by his father, and Nathan knew at once that it was a secret list, and that after he had finished reading it he would probably wish he hadn't, as he was continually pained by the memory of a love letter he had found in a box in the basement, written to his father by a girl who had once been Nathan's favorite baby-sitter. He lay on his stomach in the space where there was no longer a great, oaken desk and read what his father had set down. The handwriting was neat and restrained, as though Dr. Shapiro had been angry while he wrote.

"RESOLUTIONS," Nathan read: "1. I will never again

raise my voice with my children, or threaten them with the back of my hand. 2. I will not think ill of any man or woman, for no one could possibly be motivated by more trivial or more venal concerns than I. 3. I will cease calling my father and mother by their first names, and will strive to regain what I lost when they became Milton and Flo to me. That is, I will love my parents. 4. I will not claim to have read books that I have not read, or to have been borne out in predictions that I never made. 5. I will cease to infect Nathan with a debilitating love of facts, nor will I pursue them myself with greed and possessiveness, as I have heretofore. 6. I will be a better father. 7. I will listen to Bartók every morning, and to Mozart before I sleep. 8. I will lay aside all ambitions save the one I have cherished since the age of nineteen, when I made my first list of ten resolutions—to love and understand art, sport, science, literature, and music, and to become, someday, a true Renaissance Man. 9. I will not throw away this list."

In the midst of feeling sick to his stomach, and faintly horrified as by the glimpses given in his father's medical texts of the inner human body, the thought that Dr. Shapiro had already broken number nine was of some small comfort to Nathan. He gathered up the paper in his hands and himself crushed it, bit it, tore it in two. The telephone rang, and from the soft, interrogative sound of Ricky's voice in the kitchen he guessed that it was Dr. Shapiro calling. In a minute he would have to tell his father something, something his father would never forget because it would be the first thing Nathan said to him under these new and remarkable circumstances. Nathan hoped, he prayed very quickly to God, rocking back and forth on his knees, that his father would break all eight of the others as well, that he would continue to spank his sons, fall asleep with the radio playing Harry Belafonte and Doris Day, memorize the altitudes of the mountains of the world. None of these things seemed to Nathan to be of the slightest importance, and yet they had caused Dr. Shapiro to drive himself from the house where he had dwelt for so many years as a kind of adored, only occasionally dangerous giant, an intelligent, dexterous bear with a vast repertoire of tricks. Nathan could see from the list that Dr. Shapiro didn't know of the constant delight that his sons had taken in him or of the legends and fables that had grown up around his name. How impossible was the life of a father! thought Nathan. The best man in the world could fill a thousand pages with fine resolutions and still feel forced to leave his home in shame.

"Listen, Dad," said Nathan when he picked up the phone, throwing himself across his father's abandoned side of the bed, "I've been thinking. And really. You could come home any time you want to."

"I know that," said Dr. Shapiro.

"You were a good father, Dad," said Nathan, clutching tight the torn little ball of yellow paper. "You were the best father in the world."

"Thanks," said Dr. Shapiro, but he said it abstractedly, a little too fast, as though it were only a reply, as though his mind were on other more difficult, more wondrous things.

ADMIRALS

Nathan jammed his sneakers against the back of his father's seat and listened, eager and miserable, to the opening notes of the song on the car radio. He had no idea. His father had been quizzing him for as long as he could remember, and as a result Nathan knew the presidents of the United States (in order), the capitals of all fifty states, the provinces of Canada and the nations of Europe and *their* capitals (including Vaduz), the great inventions and their inventors, the major rivers of the world in order of length, famous black and Jewish Americans and their achievements, gods and heroes of ancient Greece, planets and moons of the solar system, as well as two dozen common phobias, including pantophobia, the fear of everything.

Unfortunately, the topic of the day was rock-and-roll music, and the quiz was for the benefit of Anne, Dr. Shapiro's girlfriend, the play lady from the children's hospital where Nathan's father was the psychiatrist. They were on their way to Annapolis (the capital of Maryland), to stay in a motel, even though Annapolis was only half an hour from Ellicott City, where Nathan, his brother, and their mother lived. It had been raining lightly all morning, the air was chilly for May, and Nathan felt a kind of dread of this false vacation. Dr. Shapiro turned up the volume on the radio and glanced over his shoulder at Nathan, then looked at Anne to make sure that she was paying attention.

"O.K.," said Dr. Shapiro, slowly rolling one hand in the air, as though guiding Nathan into a tight parking space. "Who is this?"

"David Bowie," said Ricky, Nathan's little brother. He arched forward to pat Anne on the top of her head, which was just visible to the boys in the backseat. Ricky—seven, affectionate, ill-tempered, and wild—had seen David Bowie once on television, dressed like a Navajo from Jupiter, and had been greatly impressed.

"Quiet, Ricky," said Dr. Shapiro. "Nathan?"

Since his parents' divorce, a year and a half ago, Nathan had become interested in rock-and-roll, but aside from songs by the Beatles, which he knew fairly well, and a few by the Rolling Stones, he wasn't much good at this topic. For a moment, running the names of random bands and singers through his mind, Nathan panicked, and his knees began to ache from the pressure he was exerting against his father's seat, until it occurred to him that this was a new kind of quiz. This time his father didn't know the correct answer any more than he did. He could give any name at all.

"Eric Clapton," said Nathan in an offhand way, watching the back of his father's head, then, in a burst of fresh alarm, looking to see if Anne was going to call his bluff. She was younger than his father, and he remembered with a start her having told him that the Buffalo Springfield had played at her homecoming in college.

"Eric Clapton?" said his father. "O.K.! That's amazing, isn't it, Anne?" She smiled. "Couldn't have been more than a dozen bars before he got it."

"That's great," said Anne, turning to smile at Nathan. Anne was very nice, Nathan reminded himself, and then felt guilty because he had to remind himself. He'd always liked Anne—had loved her, in fact, when she was just the play lady at his father's work. He and Ricky had spent entire days down in her playroom, gluing together Popsicle sticks and weaving multicolored pot holders that they brought home to their mother, and Anne would buy them Chinese lunches and comic books. But ever since she was his father's girlfriend, Nathan had come to suspect all of her former friendliness. He shunned her hugs and sat apart from her.

"It's David Bowie," said Ricky. "Ask me, Dad. Ask me."

"David Bowie," said Dr. Shapiro. "Get out of here."

They passed a sign for Annapolis.

"Chuck lives in Annapolis," said Ricky. "Mom says."

"Who's Chuck?" said their father.

Without knowing exactly why, Nathan hit Ricky on the arm, hard—much harder than he had intended to, really—and Ricky began to cry, then stopped and looked at Nathan, his forehead wrinkled and red.

"Um—a doo-doo head," said Ricky, valiantly turning silly. "Chuck, buck, duck, muck, luck."

Then the song was over, and Nathan's heart sank as he realized that the disk jockey in just a moment would identify the singer, and as Ricky arrived, with a gasp, at the end of his incantation. "Fuck," he whispered behind his hand. He stared blankly at Nathan for an instant, then smiled in horror and delight, his eyes still full of tears.

"We're there," said Anne, and switched off the radio.

Nathan's mother had had four boyfriends since the divorce, and, until Chuck, Nathan had liked them all. The first three boyfriends—all of them—wore beards and glasses, like Nathan's father, and drove calm, square foreign cars. They'd tried very hard to make friends with Nathan, and so he had tried, too; there were ballgames and bats' jaws and discussions of science. Each time, Nathan felt sad when the boyfriend stopped calling and didn't come to dinner anymore, though not as sad as his mother. Of the many new spectacles the divorce had created—his mother, in a suit, happily leaving for work in the morning, Nathan fixing their dinner with the radio blaring—the most disturbing was that of their mother crying, which she hadn't done even at the death of their grandfather but which now they had seen ten times at least.

And now Chuck, a small-plane pilot, was pushing their mother to even greater extremes of emotion. He had an Italian car, with only two seats. On Friday nights when Chuck broke dates, their mother sank into jealous despair, and spent the evening devouring an entire novel or talked on the phone to her friends for hours. She would indulge the boys with popcorn and board games and gin rummy, half-sadly smiling throughout. Very late one evening the past winter, she'd come downstairs in her boots, drawn on her coat, and gone out, returning in tears an hour later. The next morning Nathan found her sitting on the stairs, in her big bathrobe, the rolled Sunday paper lying in her lap. He reached down and took the paper from her and opened it, laughing, as if she were only absent-minded.

"Mom," he said. "Where did you go last night?"

She told him, crying; the story came out in little bursts as she held her breath between each sob. And over a breakfast at which Nathan drank coffee, and they heard Ricky's cartoons come on upstairs, as she confided to him other, less desperate tales of checking up on Chuck, he had felt himself, almost physically, growing older.

He felt it even now, with his father. Dr. Shapiro borrowed a dollar's worth of quarters from Nathan, to feed the parking meter, and Nathan trembled as, for the first time, he made his father a loan. They went into a bookstore, where they ridiculed the romance novels and took turns looking through a history of chess. Dr. Shapiro found a guidebook to the restaurants of Maryland and, having narrowed down the choices to three, allowed Nathan to decide where they would eat lunch. After studying the encapsulated reviews, Nathan settled finally on a waterfront seafood restaurant called the Bonhomme Richard, which specialized in soft-shell crabs, his father's favorite food. They left the bookstore and headed toward the bay, Anne and Ricky following along behind. The morning clouds had at last begun to scatter, the sun shone; they walked into the lobby of the Bonhomme Richard, and, in the few short moments before they ran into Chuck and some lady, Nathan saw very keenly how soon would come the day when he would be able to walk into a seafood restaurant and anticipate, like a dessert, a pale-brown cocktail. Then he saw Chuck in the lounge, helping a lady with red hair to put on her raincoat.

"It's like mine," said Ricky, just before he noticed Chuck. "Hey!"

It was. The lady wore a rubber slicker, the color of a taxicab, with a detachable hood. Chuck held out her empty left sleeve and she smiled at Ricky, as strangers often did. Nathan grabbed his little brother's arm, as gently as he could bear, and turned him toward their father and Anne, who were already disappearing into the dining room. As the boys followed after, Nathan struggled—like Orpheus and Lot's wife—against the urge to turn and look back at the handsome, mysterious airplane pilot and the lady in the child's raincoat. Finally he gave in and was irritated to see that Ricky, too, had turned to look.

"Don't look," said Nathan.

"You did," said Ricky.

They watched Chuck set an extra dollar in the little tray of money, then take the lady's arm; she looked up brightly into Chuck's face, and he blew a puff of air, ruffling her red bangs, and then they came at the boys, laughing. They were a happy couple. It was sad. Nathan thought of a time, long ago in Richmond, Virginia, when his parents had stood in the doorway of his bedroom, looking into each other's faces and at little Nathan dancing naked on his bed, their arms around each other's waists. Nathan's father had called his mother Rosie, the only time ever, and Nathan had stopped dancing. "Rosie!" he had cried.

"Here's Dad," said Ricky.

Their father approached, his hands outspread, one eyebrow lifted in mock annoyance.

"We're coming," said Nathan. "Here we come."

"What did you see?" said Dr. Shapiro.

They sat down and Nathan opened his menu. At first he was too upset to do anything but stare at the descriptions of all the different dishes. Colored drawings of fish swam around the menu's border—haddock, cod, flat flounder and sole, and the ugly fish that wasn't a dolphin but was called a dolphin. He felt—as though suddenly and irrevocably he were his mother's ambassador to Annapolis and to the whole world—as if he were going to cry.

"Look," said Ricky. "Admirals."

They'd been seated in a part of the restaurant that stretched out over the water, at a table beside a window. Across the room, along another row of windows, was the bar, just now entirely taken up by naval officers in white uniforms, nearly two dozen, a flock of admirals. Their upside-down hats littered the top of the bar; the lunchtime sun fell across their square shoulders and lit up their dazzling coats. All the men looked handsome and happy, their cocktails flashed in their hands, and Nathan cherished the elegant lime in a gin-and-tonic.

"What are you having, Nathan?" said his father.

"How much can it cost?" he asked, since the only things that sounded good were expensive. Nathan preferred, as a rule, to order the dishes with the most ingredients and with the most adjectives applied to them. His father tossed his head and waved away Nathan's question.

"You can have whatever you want," he said. It was what he always said, and it was one of the four thousand things for which Nathan adored him.

The waiter came and did his waiter's tricks for Ricky, snapping out a napkin, mixing Ricky's chocolate milk right at the table, pouring milk into the glass at first from just above it, then from a great height, then dipping and rising again, as though the milk were a white rubber band. Dr. Shapiro ordered soft-shell crabs, then rose from the table and went to find a pay telephone.

This was another recent and disturbing phenomenon. Nathan knew that his father liked to listen to the boys' orders, to express his ceremonial approval or surprise. But in the past couple of months Dr. Shapiro had begun to disappear suddenly—to go off looking for pay phones in restaurants and department stores, preoccupied by "keeping in touch" with his patients' parents, with the hospital, with his Pakistani colleagues. He telephoned so regularly and resignedly that Nathan came to associate these dutiful calls with the twice-weekly ones the boys got from him, which Ricky seemed to enjoy but which Nathan (and, he suspected, his father) found both difficult and somehow unjust.

Anne and Nathan looked at each other and shared a sarcastic smile, as though Dr. Shapiro's new telephone mania were only ridiculous. Then the sarcasm went out of Anne's face. She looked after her boyfriend with a furrowed brow, then turned to Nathan and tried to smile again. It was as though, for a moment, she had laid down her mask and told him that it was O.K. to worry, that, indeed, something abnormal was happening around them. In that moment Nathan felt that he loved her. But then she smiled.

Ricky, ordering the fried jumbo shrimps (he was in the throes of a mad shrimp phase), knocked over the entire glass of chocolate milk. His apologies were so irritable and sincere that a few of the shining admirals across the room looked over and laughed, grandly; the glass, after all, had not broken. Ricky smiled and calmed down. When their father came back, pulling at his beard, Ricky leaned toward him.

"Dad, the admirals laughed at me," he said. "All the way from across the room."

Anne took Nathan's hand and whispered into his ear.

"It wasn't Eric Clapton," she told him, blushing.

"Oh," said Nathan, watching his father look out emptily and awestruck over the platinum water, as though a great, gay ocean liner were passing by.

"It was the Rolling Stones," she said. "It was 'We Love You.'"

As they left the restaurant, it began to sprinkle again, and they hurried through the streets from shop to shop. One, full of old tables and chairs, stood beside another that was full of artistic toys—painted clowns, dancers on cords, wooden trains in the shapes of ducks and ducklings. So they split up. Lately Dr. Shapiro and Anne had become interested in old furniture, and although Nathan had tried for a little while to share their interest, as an adult would— to examine the splinters of wear in a wicker seat, to see how tables could be important—it was not easy to do, so when Ricky failed to spot the toyshop immediately, Nathan pointed it out to him. He waited for Ricky's shouts of discovery, then feigned acquiescence when his father ordered him to escort his brother into the shop.

They quickly discovered that most of the artistic toys were in the windows, and that it was really just an ordinary toy store, with fine, ordinary toys. Ricky was overjoyed. He shot at Nathan with a ray gun that threw sparks and whined, put on a small diving mask and hooted through the snorkel, got all the battery-powered toys to crawl and beep across the table on which they were displayed, exclaiming happily when they crashed into each other. Whenever Nathan went into toy stores these days, a confusion of feelings came over him, and now he stood, hands in pockets, beside a glass case of miniature knights, soldiers, and farm animals, absently watching his brother cause toy disaster.

At home, with their mother, Ricky did little harm to fixtures or vases, but his mood was black, and he kicked and shrieked; with their father he was festive and wily, and full of comments, but he couldn't be trusted near anything valuable, and sometimes the sturdiest appliances came to pieces under his hand. Their mother's nerves were shattered, like their father's pipes and tumblers. When Ricky was not around, he was discussed in a manner that made Nathan uneasy, because the assumption seemed to be that Ricky had some kind of problem, or would soon be a problem—which, when Nathan thought about it for a minute, almost certainly meant that he, too, was a problem, only older.

"Nate! Nate!" said Ricky, from somewhere at the front

of the toy store. Nathan looked one last time at the toy horse and crusader, reared up on their swath of metal turf—the only thing in the store that he even faintly coveted—then went to find his brother. Ricky stood on tiptoe, clutching the top of the low wood partition that protected the display of untouchable toys in the front window; he was looking past all the duckies and dancers to something in the street outside.

First Nathan saw the fabulous car. It was like a color-plate in the cumbersome book he'd been given for his eleventh birthday, *The History of the Motor Car*—a Cord, or a Duesenberg, or a Daimler, or one of those other extinct breeds of car that looked like small, wheeled mansions, with curtains, doorknobs, tiny lamps, the running boards like long verandas. And, as in the illustrations Nathan had gazed at, on the toilet or under the covers of his bed for hours at a time, there was something airless and artificial about the car—something as dead and impossible as the reconstructed skeletons of Allosaurus and Triceratops in a museum. There was a story, famous in their family—even Anne knew it—about Nathan at age four asking his parents which had come first, the dinosaurs or the old-fashioned cars. It still sometimes seemed to him that the things that had happened before he was born—Pearl Harbor, hieroglyphics, catapults, the day his parents fell in love—were equally ancient and interesting, cryptic and gone.

"It's a millionaire," said Ricky.

"It's a playboy," said Nathan.

The man stood in the light rain with one foot on the running board of his car, staring off toward the distant bay.

He wore a blue blazer with a coat of arms on the breast pocket, white trousers, no socks, blue sailor's sneakers. In one hand he casually held a briar, and in the other a gold lighter. He neither slouched nor stood erect, and Nathan immediately adjusted his own posture to match the play-boy's, but it was the man's short silver hair that Nathan admired most, and the perfect wrinkles at the corners of his eyes, and his slight smile.

"See that silver hair?" said Nathan. "When I'm old I want to have hair like that."

"It's gray," said Ricky. "Can that car go a hundred miles an hour?"

"Any car can go a hundred miles an hour," said Nathan the older brother. "You're just supposed to look at that car. It doesn't go anywhere."

Their father appeared on the sidewalk in front of the toy store, and he and the playboy said hello.

"Dad's talking to him," said Ricky.

"You're allowed to talk to guys like that when they stand there with their cars," said Nathan. "They like it."

Dr. Shapiro walked over to the man with silver hair and gestured at his car. The man nodded politely but didn't smile. Beside him their father looked small, wet, bald, and faintly sloppy, and the fluttery hand he held out toward the vaulting fender of the car seemed to try—and fail—to grasp, to clutch. The playboy said something and then looked away again. Nathan saw in that instant that his father was a man whom a playboy would shun. Then a woman carrying shopping bags came toward the men—a television blonde, wearing an ash-gray trenchcoat and lots of makeup; she was very tall, with beautiful teeth. She twirled her umbrella over her head and it shot drops around her like a firework of water.

"An actress," said Ricky, pinching Nathan's arm.

The playboy nodded again to Dr. Shapiro, then went around to open the door for the actress, who gave the playboy a look that Nathan recognized. He had seen his mother give this look to Chuck, and she had no doubt once given it to his father—this look which, now that he recognized it, seemed to convey everything that, Nathan imagined, constituted sexual desire, a look of soft, distrustful frankness, wide- and wet-eyed. And then they got in and drove away, the car sweeping out of the parking space and into the street without a sound, without a squeal, like a sailboat.

"You lied," said Ricky. "It does go."

"Look at Dad," said Nathan.

Dr. Shapiro stood watching the fabulous car disappear for a moment, wiping the rain from his glasses, his head slightly turned away, as though he were listening to the couple's dwindling laughter.

"He's only a psychiatrist," said Ricky.

"Here he comes," said Nathan. He grabbed Ricky and pulled him into the board-game aisle. When their father came in, he was soaking wet, and he bought his sons several bright things that they had not asked for.

That night in the motel room, as he lay beside his brother, Nathan listened to the people sleeping around him; Ricky snored delicately. Nathan could hear the hum of the ice machine in the corridor, could hear his father's wrist-watch ticking on the night table, and the general, half-imaginary murmur that all motels emit at night. Anne had drawn the curtains; the room was so completely black that Nathan began to see bright colors, luminous Persian rugs. Lately he suffered from night anxieties, and although he would think and think about everything in his life that might be upsetting him—library fines, his recent failure to pass the parallel-bars exam, his fear of high school—he couldn't determine what it was that kept him awake, with a stomach ache, night after night. It was as though he were trying to remember the answer to one of his father's questions. He rolled onto his back, the motel sheets crackled, and, after a while, he began to drift, and the colors faded from his eyes. Ricky coughed in his sleep once, angrily. Then, in the instant before Nathan went under, a picture came into his mind. He lay like Moses in a little basket, floating among the bulrushes, and his parents stood on the bank above him, their arms around each other's waists, looking down. They were singing to him. "We love you," they sang.

THE
HALLOWEEN PARTY

———

Whenever Nathan Shapiro regarded Eleanor Parnell, it was like looking at a transparent overlay in the *World Book Encyclopedia*. In his mind he would flip back and forth from today's deep-voiced, black-haired, chain-smoking, heavy-breasted woman in a red sheath dress or tight dungarees, gracefully working the cork from another bottle of pink California wine, to the vague, large, friendly woman in plaids who had fed him year after year on Cokes and deviled-ham sandwiches, whose leaves he had raked for seven autumns now, and who still lay somewhere underneath the new Eleanor, like the skeleton of a frog beneath the bright chaos of its circulatory system.

It was only since Nathan had turned fourteen and found himself privy to the reckless conversation of divorcées—of those half-dozen funny, sad women with whom his mother had surrounded herself—that he had discovered Eleanor Parnell to be a woman of bad habits and of enterprises that ended in disaster. They said that she baked and consumed marijuana desserts, and that she liked to spend Christmas Eve playing blackjack in Las Vegas, alone. She drove her scarlet Alfa Romeo with the abandon of someone who, as

Mrs. Shapiro pointed out, had always been very unlucky.

When she was hardly older than Nathan was now, Eleanor had spent two triumphant years on the L.P.G.A. tour; then she'd fallen from a horse and broken her left elbow. Nathan had seen her trophies once, in a glass cabinet up in Eleanor and Major Ray's bedroom. Her real-estate company went down under a hailstorm of lawsuits and threats of criminal prosecution, which Nathan and his mother had read about in the Huxley *New Idea* and even, eventually, in *The Washington Post*. Cayenne, her New Orleans-style restaurant in Huxley Mall, closed after only a few months. And there had been a pale little baby, a redhead named Sullivan, who lived so briefly that Ricky, Nathan's little brother, did not even remember him.

All these tales of misfortune, all the melancholy under Eleanor's eyes and around her mouth, had the surprising—to Nathan—effect of causing him to fall helplessly in love. It began one August when, after a hiatus of several years, he resumed his ancient habit of visiting the Parnells' house every day, for soft drinks and conversation with Eleanor. He was driven to her, at first, simply by loneliness and by the sadness of boredom. Ricky was gone—he had gone to live in Boston with their father the previous spring—and during the tedious, spectacular afternoons of August the house was distressingly empty. All month, Mrs. Shapiro, who was a nurse, had to work late on the ward, so Nathan ate dinner with his friend Edward St. John and Edward's bohemian family more often than usual, and he was glad to spend the last afternoons of the summer down the street at the Parnells'. Major Ray—Major Raymond Parnell, of

Galveston, Texas—did not get home from the base until seven o'clock, and Nathan would sit in the kitchen until Major Ray's boisterous arrival, watching Eleanor smoke cigarettes and squeeze lemons into her diet Coke, of which she drank sixty ounces a day—enough, as Major Ray often declared, to reanimate a dead body. She would ask Nathan for his opinions on hair styles, decorating, ecology, religion, and music, and he would offer them only after a good deal of consideration, in an airy, humorous, pedantic tone of voice, which he borrowed, without knowing it, from his father. Eleanor had treated him without condescension when he was a little boy, and she now listened to him with an intentness that was both respectful and amused, as though she half expected him to tell her something new.

Nathan's love for Eleanor followed hard on the heels of his long-awaited and disastrous growth spurt, and it wrenched him every bit as much, until his chest ached from the sudden and irregular expansion of his feelings. In the mirror the sight of his heavy-rimmed eyeglasses and unfortunate complexion; of the new, irregular largeness of his body, of his suddenly big—his fat—stomach, would send him off on giddy binges of anxiety. He ate sweet snacks and slept badly and jumped at loud sounds. The sight of Eleanor's red Alfa Romeo—the sight of any red car—disturbed him. He was filled with deep compassion for animals and children, in particular for Nickel Boy, the Parnells' dog, a sensitive, courtly old beagle. In fact, Nathan spoke at length to Nickel Boy about his feelings for Eleanor, even though he knew that talking to a dog was not really talking but, as he had read in Psychology Today, simply making a lot of comforting sounds in order to secrete some enzyme that would lower his own blood pressure and slow his pulse.

Every night before he switched off the lamp, and every morning when he awoke, he took out the collection of photographs of Eleanor Parnell he had pilfered from his mother's album and looked deeply into each of them, trying to speak to Eleanor with the telepathy of love. In his freshman-English class they arrived at the writing of poetry, and Nathan, startled into action, composed haiku, limericks, odes, and cinquains to Eleanor, as well as an acrostic sonnet, the first letters of whose lines daringly spelled out E-L-E-A-N-O-R P-A-R-N-E-L L whenever, in these poems, he referred to her directly, he called her Jennifer—like "Eleanor" a dactyl.

On the Saturday before the start of his freshman year of high school, as Nathan wandered home through the woods from Edward's house, trying to walk erect, he saw Eleanor under the tulip poplars, in a battered pith helmet, wildly shooting down wasps' nests with the pistol nozzle of a garden hose. Great golden, malevolent wasps had been something of a problem all summer, but after all the rain in July they proliferated and flew into the houses at suppertime.

"Is it working?" called Nathan, trotting toward her. One of the things he loved about Eleanor was her inventiveness, however doomed.

"Oh, no," Eleanor said. As soon as she glimpsed Nathan she began to laugh, and the stream of water shivered and fell to the ground. Her laugh, which was the first thing Nathan remembered noticing about Eleanor, had always been odd—raucous and dark, like a cartoon magpie's or spider's—but lately it had come for Nathan to be invested with the darkness of sex and the raucousness of having survived misfortune. She had been in the sun too long, and her face was bright red. "No one was supposed to see me doing this. Do you think this is a bad idea? They look pretty pissed off. Major Ray thought this wasn't a good idea." Major Ray did not appreciate Eleanor.

"I disagree," said Nathan, gazing up at the treetops, where the wasps had hung their cities of paper. A dense golden cloud of wasps wavered around them. "There's a lot less of them now."

"Do you think so?" said Eleanor. She took off her hat and stared upward. Her bangs clung to her damp, sunburned forehead.

"Yes," said Nathan. "I guess you drowned them. Or maybe the impact kills them. Of the water." The cloud of wasps widened and descended. "Uh, Eleanor. Could I— Maybe I should try it."

"All right," said Eleanor. She handed him the squirting, hissing nozzle and then, solemnly, the pith helmet, all the while keeping an eye on the insects and biting her lip. Almost immediately Nathan got the feeling that a blanket, or a net, was about to fall on him. Eleanor jumped backward with a cry, and Nathan was left to fight off the wasps with his lunatic weapon, which he did for fifteen valiant seconds. Then he ran, with Eleanor behind him. He tore around the front of the Parnells' house, crossed the front lawn, and ran out onto Les Adieux Circle. At the center of the cul-de-sac lay a round patch of grass, planted with a single, frail oak tree. No one on the street knew who was supposed to mow this island and so it generally went unmown, and, according to the local children's legend, it harbored a family of field rats. He and Eleanor fell into the weeds, and Nathan's eyeglasses, which were photosensitive and had darkened in the afternoon sunshine, flew from his face. Dazzled, frightened, he rolled laughing in her rosy arms, and they embraced like a couple of fortunate castaways. Then, his heart pounding, he scrambled to his knees and sought the comforting weight, the protection of his glasses.

Of the four stings that Nathan received, three were on his thigh and one was on his shoulder. Eleanor took him into the house, up the stairs, and into the bedroom, where blue laundry lay folded on the big bed and where Eleanor's gold trophies, like so many miniature Mormon temples, sat shining dimly in their cabinet. Then she led him into the bathroom, lowered the lid onto the toilet, and sat him down.

"Roll up your cutoffs, Nathan," she said. She found a box of baking soda and mixed a little with some tap water in the plastic bathroom cup. Nathan pulled upward on the frazzled leg of his shorts and tried to keep from crying. She knelt beside him to daub his pale, fat, blistered thigh. Nathan flinched, but the paste was cool, and he was overcome with gratitude. He didn't know what to do, and so he stared at the parting of her hair, at Eleanor's miraculous scalp, white and fine as polished wood.

"I guess Major Ray was right," said Eleanor. "It wasn't such a hot idea." She cackled nervously, and it was a relief to Nathan to see that she also felt that something weird was happening—such a relief that he began to cry, although he hated crying more than anything else in the world.

"Oh, Jesus, does it hurt, honey?" Eleanor said. "I'm sorry, I'm sorry. Does it hurt?"

This expression of concern made Nathan inordinately happy, and he tried to tell her it didn't hurt a bit, but he was too miserable to speak. He was frightened by the zeal of his crying, but it felt too good to stop. So he covered his face and hee-hawed like a child.

Eleanor stopped ministering to his wasp stings and sat back on her heels, regarding Nathan. A different kind of concern entered her face, and all at once she looked very sad. "What's the matter, Nathan?" she said.

But Nathan told no one, not even Edward, to whom he generally confided all his ludicrous amours. The two boys had supported and amused one another through a long series of fanciful loves, but until now the objects of their affections had always been unattainable, unlikely, and laughable: a prom queen, a postwoman, the earth-sciences teacher Miss Patocki, or the disturbing Sabina McFay, Edward's nineteen-year-old neighbor, who was half Vietnamese and rode a motorcycle. Not so Eleanor Parnell; she was unattainable and farfetched, but she was not at all laughable, and Nathan said nothing to Edward about her.

When he learned, from his mother, that he had been invited to the Parnells' Halloween party, he was flattered and struck with fear, and during the abject, optimistic weeks that followed he resolved to declare his feelings to Eleanor Parnell once and for all at this party. For ten days his head was filled with whispered, intricate repartee.

At dusk on Halloween, just as the youngest and most carefully chaperoned of the demons and nurses and mice were beginning to make their rounds, Nathan and Edward were standing in the living room of the Shapiros' house, drawing pictures with colored pencils onto Mrs. Shapiro's arms, back, and shoulders. Nathan's mother sat on a horse-hide ottoman, in blue fishnet tights, blue high-heeled shoes, and a strapless Popsicle-blue bathing suit, laughing and complaining that the boys were pressing too hard as they drew anchors, hearts, thunderbolts, and snakes across her skin. The boys dipped the tips of the pencils into a jar of water, which made the colors run rich. As the drawings began to predominate over unmarked patches of skin, Nathan put his crimson pencil down and stepped back, as if to admire their handiwork.

"I think that's enough tattoos, Mom," he said.

"Is that so?" said his mother.

"Personally," said Edward, inspecting her, "I think a big, you know, triumphant eagle, with a javelin in its claw, right here under your neck, would look really cool, Mrs. Shapiro. Rose."

"That sounds fine, Edward," said Mrs. Shapiro.

Nathan looked at his friend, who began to paint a gray, screaming eagle. Nothing about his voice or studious little face indicated that he felt anything but the enthusiasm of art. As a matter of fact, his drawings were much better than Nathan's—bold, well drafted, easily recognizable; the snakes Nathan had drawn looked kind of like sewing needles, or flattened teaspoons.

"If you think about it," said Edward, in the careful but dazed way he had of propounding his many insights, "the symbol of our country is a really warlike symbol."

"Hmm," said Mrs. Shapiro. "Isn't that interesting?"

When her costume was finally complete, and Nathan regarded her in all her fiery, gay motley, his heart sank, and he was seized with doubts about the costume he'd decided on. After much indecision and agonized debate with Edward, whose father was an avant-garde artist, Nathan had decided upon a *conceptual* Halloween costume. He had made a coat hanger into a wire ring that sat like a diadem on his brow, bent the end of it so that it would stand up over the back of his head, then made a small loop into which he could screw a light bulb. When he wore this contraption the light bulb seemed to hang suspended a few inches above him, and the wire was, in a dim room, practically invisible. He was going to the Parnells' Halloween party, in Edward's excited formulation, as a guy in the process of having a good idea for a costume.

The whole notion now struck Nathan as childish, and anemic, and it bothered him that the light bulb would never actually be lit up, and would just bob there, gray and dull, atop his head, as though he were really going to Eleanor's party as a guy in the process of having a *bad* idea for a costume. The truth was that Nathan felt so keenly how plain, how squat and clumsy he had become—his belly had begun to strain against the ribbed elastic of his new gym shorts, and his mother had received his last school pictures with a fond, motherly, devastating sigh—that he regretted having passed up the opportunity of concealing himself, if only for one night, in the raiment of a robot or a king.

"Cool," said Edward, standing up straight and blowing gently on the eagle tattoo.

Mrs. Shapiro rose from the ottoman, went to the chrome mirror that had been one of his parents' last joint purchases, and seemed greatly pleased by the apparition that she saw there. She hadn't wanted them to illustrate her face, and now it rose pale and almost shockingly bare from her shoulders. "You did a great job," she said. "I like the hula girl, Edward," she added, looking down at her right biceps.

"Make a muscle," he said. He went to the mirror and took hold of her right arm and wrist. Nathan followed.

"Flex your arm," said Edward.

Mrs. Shapiro flexed her arm. Nathan leaned over his friend's shoulder to watch the hula girl do a rudimentary bump and grind. He looked around for something to stand on, to get a better view, and his glance fell upon the matching chrome wastebasket, which stood beside the mirror, but when he balanced himself on its edge and peered down at the dancing tattoo the wastebasket immediately gave way. Nathan's eyeglasses, which for weeks he'd been meaning to tighten, slipped from his face, and when he fell he landed on them with a gruesome crunch.

"Oh, no," said Mrs. Shapiro. "Not again."

"I'm sorry, Mom," said Nathan.

"Are you all right? Did you hurt yourself?"

Edward, laughing, held out his hand to Nathan to pull him to his feet.

"You're insane, Dr. Lester," he said.

"You're deranged, Madame LaFarge," said Nathan, automatically. He looked at his friend and his tattooed mother gazing down upon him with a kind of mild, perfunctory concern. They turned to one another and laughed. A barrage of miniature-demon knocks rang out against the front door of the house. Nathan passed a hand before his eyes, blinked, and shook his head.

"I can see," he said flatly.

After Edward went home, he and his mother sat down at the kitchen table that smelled of 409 and called Ricky in Boston, to find out how his trick-or-treating had gone and to tell him that Nathan could see without his glasses. This was a development that ophthalmologists had been calling for since Nathan was five and had donned his first little owlish pair of horn-rims. Though its coming to pass was certainly something of a shock, it did not surprise him, especially now, when the behavior of his body was so continually shocking, and when so many of the ancient fixtures of his life—his slight form, his smooth face, his father and brother—were vanishing one by one.

Anne, his stepmother, answered the phone but went immediately to find Ricky, as she always did, and it occurred to Nathan for the first time that he was never particularly kind to her. He looked at the receiver, wishing he could run after her, and waited for Ricky to pick up his extension. His brother had just come in from trick-or-treating and was almost delirious with sated greed.

"Almond Roca, Nate!" he exulted. "Popcorn balls that are orange!"

"You can't eat the ones that aren't wrapped. Throw away the popcorn balls."

"Why?"

"Razor blades," said Nathan. He missed his brother so badly that it made him nervous to speak to Ricky on the phone. They talked to each other three times a week, but they could never generate any real silliness, and Nathan, in spite of himself, was always irritable and mocking, or stern.

"Yeah," Ricky said excitedly. "Halloween razor blades. Oh, my God, Nate, someone gave me raisin bread! *Raisin bread*, Nate!"

"I don't believe it," said Nathan. "Ricky, guess what?"

"I bet it was Mrs. Gilette. Hey, what are you going to be? Galactus?"

Ricky had spent his entire life waiting for Nathan to dress as Galactus, the World Eater, for Halloween, which was something Nathan a long time ago had said he was going to do, not dreaming that Ricky would never forget it, and would even come to regard it as the greatest and most magical of all the magical promises that his older brother had ever broken. In this instance Nathan felt more guilty than usual about having to tell Ricky the sorry truth, and he swiveled around in his chair so that his mother wouldn't be able to see his face.

"I'm going as a guy in the process of having a good idea for a costume," he mumbled.

"Huh?"

"You wouldn't understand it."

"I don't understand it because it's dumb," said Ricky. "I can tell it must be dumb."

"Go to hell," said Nathan.

"Nathan," said Mrs. Shapiro.

"Go to hell *you*," said Ricky.

"Guess what? I can see without my glasses." Nathan spun around to face his mother, and she looked at him with mild amazement.

"You mean you never have to wear them ever again?" said Ricky. Absently he added, "Now you won't be so ugly."

This thought had not occurred to Nathan. He heard the sound of a plastic bag full of candy bars being rummaged around in and felt that he had exhausted Ricky's attention span, just when he most needed to speak to him. This incompleteness was why Nathan had first come to hate talking on the telephone to his father, in the days of his parents' trial separation. Ricky tore open a wrapper and began to chew. Bit-O-Honey, from the sound of it. Nathan pictured his brother surrounded by candy, lying in his fancy bedroom in Boston on his bed shaped like a racing car. It was a big bedroom, with a large, empty alcove at the back, which Ricky claimed to be afraid of entering. Nathan imagined the Boston Halloween night through the windows in the dark alcove as Ricky would see it from his speeding bed. "The big brother is always uglier," Ricky said.

"I know you're only teasing me," said Nathan. As he had several times before, he felt very far away from his brother just then, as he felt far from Anne and his father and mother and everyone he knew, isolated in his love and anxiety, but for the first time the void around him seemed to offer a new perspective, as though he were standing safely on top of a house in the midst of a great flood. He had no desire to return Ricky's insults. He looked at Mrs. Shapiro, who, although she didn't know what Ricky had said, nodded her head. "I know I'm not ugly," said Nathan.

"No," said the sleepy little boy in Boston, flowing off away from Nathan on his bed of sweets. "You have nice shoulders."

It was as Nathan walked with his mother through the woods to the Parnells' house that he began to feel distinctly altered. These trees were going to be cut down soon, to make way for three new houses, and as he strode, barefaced, across the little wood, there seemed a particular clarity to the starlit Halloween air, a sharpness that hitherto he had only smelled, and the sight of the world struck him with the austere flavor of smoke and dead leaves. Up the street the beam of a child's flashlight tumbled to the ground, igniting the red oak leaves that littered the Parnells' lawn, and then flew upward, illuminating the bare tops of previously invisible trees.

"I can't believe it," said Nathan. "I must be cured."

"You look very nice without your glasses," said his mother. "You look like your father."

"Dad wears glasses."

"He didn't always," she said. She shivered in her coat, which was made from rabbits and had been the gift of Humberto, the Brazilian professional soccer player she had dated last winter.

"Do you think my concept is stupid, Mom?"

"I just don't really understand it, Nathan," said his mother. "I never really understand your jokes. I'm sure lots of people will think it's hilarious."

They came to the short incline of yellow lawn which rose to the cedar planks of the Parnells' front porch, and which was transected by a crooked line of stepping-stones that led to the shallow goldfish pond beside the front door. Major Ray had been stationed for five years in Yokohama during the sixties, and the Parnells had returned with a houseful of Japanese things. The carved pumpkin shared the porch with a stone lamp shaped like a pointed Japanese house, and as Nathan and his mother stepped up to the front door—you could already hear them inside, dozens of laughing adults—it struck him that a jack-o'-lantern was truly a lantern. His last thought before Eleanor threw open the door was an idea for a science-fiction novel in which the denizens of a distant world furnished their lives with various giant vegetables, carving out their beds, dressing in long, curly peels, illuminating their homes with the light of pumpkins. Then the door flew open. In all his anxiety over his own wardrobe, in all the editing and revision of the tortured sentence he intended that night jauntily to pronounce to Eleanor, he had forgotten to wonder about what she might wear, and he found himself taken completely by surprise.

Nathan had been prey, of course, to night fantasies of Eleanor Parnell. He concocted these happy narratives of seduction with the same thoroughness he brought to all his imaginary projects, such as Davor, the Golden Planet, and the vast turnpike, each of its rest stops and motor courts carefully named, that he had once mapped across two hundred pages of his loose-leaf notebook. He had envisioned Mrs. Parnell in all manner of empty rooms, and on desert beaches, and under a remote lean-to in the Far West, but during these trysts she remained demurely clothed. (At those crucial moments when Eleanor began to remove her garments, Nathan's vision tended to falter.) But he had never imagined her in a black leather bikini, black cape, black boots, and black visor with a great pointed pair of black leather ears.

"I'm Batman," Eleanor said, giving Nathan a dry kiss on the cheek. "You look wonderful," she said to Mrs. Shapiro. She stepped back to examine Nathan, and her eyes narrowed within their moon-shaped black windows. "Nathan, you're a—You're a lamp. You're a lamppost."

"Oh, no," said Mrs. Shapiro.

"That's right," said Nathan the Lamppost. "Ha, ha." He could not say whether it was desire he felt for her or total, irredeemable embarrassment.

"Nathan," said his mother. "You are not a lamp. Tell her."

"Come in," said Eleanor. "We're in the Yellow Room. So what are you, Nathan?"

She drew them into the house, taking their hands in her own, as was her habit. The Yellow Room was filled, as Nathan had known it would be, with alcohol and disco music and adulthood in its most intimidating aspect. Two dozen men and women in costume—Nathan spotted a knight, a baseball player, and some sort of witch or hag—held their drinks and shouted mildly at each other over the agitated music, and five or six couples were dancing in the middle of the room. Ever since his mother had become a single woman she had increasingly involved herself, it seemed, with adults who liked to dance—a sight that for Nathan had not lost its novelty. He especially enjoyed watching the diligent men as they jogged in place.

"O.K., I give up," Eleanor said. She turned to face him and Nathan stopped dead. "No, I don't." A pinched look crossed her face as she scanned his body, and she seemed to take in for the first time the poverty of Nathan's lamentable concept. Nathan blushed and looked away, though this was partly because he feared he had already looked too many times at her breasts and at her radiant stomach.

"Are you supposed to be Thomas Edison? Is that it? Are you Thomas Alva Edison?"

Nathan forced himself to meet the humiliation of her sympathetic gaze. He opened his mouth to explain, to tell her that he was indeed the Wizard of Menlo Park, on the verge of stealing fire.

"He's a guy in the process of having a good idea for a costume," said Mrs. Shapiro, crossing her arms and shrugging her tattooed shoulders. "What do you think of that?"

"Nathan," said Eleanor, smiling at Nathan and taking his chin between the long fingers of her hand. "You're such a strange young man."

She laughed her magpie's laugh, and in her hooded eyes

Nathan read both pain and amusement, as though she already knew that he loved her. Then she turned away from him, and the two women put their arms around one another—a habit his mother had picked up from Eleanor, who had learned it from Major Ray, who put his arm around everybody. They went to the long table, draped by a black paper tablecloth, that served as the bar. Major Ray, wearing his Bruce Wayne smoking jacket, came over to hug Mrs. Shapiro. He said something to her, she laughed, and then he led her off to one side, so that Eleanor was left momentarily alone. For a moment Nathan, suffused with the careless, wild-haired courage of an inventor, contemplated Eleanor in her racy suit. He took a step toward her, then another, tentatively, gathering all his strength, as though about to throw a heavy switch that would, if his calculations were correct, bring light to a hundred cities and ten thousand darkened rooms. He was going to ask her to dance— that was all. In the few seconds before he reached her batwinged side he searched his memory for a suave line or smooth invitation from some movie, but all he could think of at that moment was *Young Mr. Lincoln.* "Eleanor," he said, "I would like to dance with you in the worst way."

Eleanor smiled, then leaned close to him and put her hand on his shoulder, her lips to his ear. For a long time she hesitated. "I know a couple of very bad ways," she said at last, "but you're too young for them, Nathan."

"I suppose so," he said, almost happily. He doffed his wire hat and set it down on the bar. There was now nothing on his face or his temples, and he felt light, almost headless, as he imagined he would feel on the brilliant evening he tried liquor for the first time. He took her hand, peacefully, and put it over his eyes, then covered her visor with his own damp palm. They stood a moment in this darkness. Then he said, "Guess who I am now."

THE
LOST WORLD

———————

One summer night not long after he turned sixteen, Nathan Shapiro drank four tall cans of Old English 800 and very soon found himself sitting in the front seat of a huge, banana-colored Ford LTD, with his friends Buster, Felix, and Tiger Montaine. They had swallowed the malt liquor while bathing in Buster French's hot tub (the Frenches were from Los Angeles) and, as a result, were driving around boiled, steaming drunk, and in various stages of undress. Buster and Felix E. still had on their scant Speedo bathing suits, Tiger Montaine wore only a black mesh tank top and one sanitary sock, and Nathan, through some combination of glee and desperation, was naked from head to toe.

Two weeks before this, his mother, in a modest and homemade little ceremony, had married a man named Ed, a kindly, balding geologist from Idaho whom she had been dating for six months. And then just this evening, an hour before Nathan went over to Buster French's house, Dr. Shapiro had telephoned jubilantly from Boston to announce the first pregnancy of his wife, Anne. Ricky, Nathan's brother, had been living in Boston for a year now, and he went on and on over the phone about the little bubble of life that had blossomed in the vial of Anne's home pregnancy test, which Ricky had taken to his room and placed between his soccer trophy and a photograph of his mother and father and Nathan standing in the wind at Nag's Head.

All of these developments, though he did his best to welcome them, had left Nathan somewhat more than normally confused. He liked his new stepfather, who had been to Antarctica and Peru and Novaya Zemlya and returned with all sorts of hair-raising tales and queer stones; in his own way he was genuinely as excited as Ricky by the prospect of a new baby; and he was old enough to regard these changes as the inevitable outward expansion, as of an empire or a galaxy, of what once had been his family. He was happy for his parents in their new lives, the way he had always been happy for them, all along, as step by step they had dismantled their marriage; and so he was looking for a reason, an excuse to feel so unmoored, at once so angry and nostalgic; and alcohol seemed to be doing the job. He had no idea of where he and his friends were going, and it was not until they had been lurching aimlessly along the empty, fragrant streets of Huxley for what seemed like hours that he understood that they were headed—as Buster French put it—to the crib of Chaya Feldman.

Buster, driving Mrs. French's car, made this declaration just as the drink, the deep velour seats, and the sweet smell of lawns flowing in through the open windows had begun to lull Nathan to sleep, and at the mention of Chaya's name Nathan sat bolt upright. Buster then called Chaya a "skeezer," which meant, as far as Nathan had been able to determine, that she was certain to permit them—all four of them—those dark liberties of which he was still very much ignorant, a notion which filled him only with wonder, and with solicitude for Chaya, whom he had known since he was six years old. She was a quiet girl, with a serious brown face and tangled hair, and her parents dressed her like a doll. He remembered her as someone who was always coming upon orphaned puppies and sparrow chicks with broken wings, in meadows and along roads where anyone else would have found nothing at all, and then trying imperfectly and with an eyedropper full of milk or sugar water to nurse them back to health. Her chief social art—until recently, at least—had been that, upon request, she could draw you an extremely realistic picture of an eyeball, with a sparkle on the iris, and fathomless pupils, and the finest tracery of veins.

They had never really been friends, but from time to time Nathan still thought about one distant afternoon when he and Chaya had somehow ended up playing together, in the fields behind the Huxley Interfaith Plexus. In the tall grass and the weeds they had played a game of Chaya's own invention, called Planet of the Birds. Nathan had been an intergalactic castaway trying to survive in a windy, grassy world, and Chaya's hair had tossed like a crest of feathers as she sang to him in a variety of cries. Chaya even claimed that when she grew up she was going to write a book set on this imaginary planet, whose name, she said, was Jadis; in the dust she scratched a map of its oceans and aeries. As with all of those blissful Sunday afternoons he had ever passed with some child with whom he never played again— every childhood has a dozen or so—his memory of this vanished afternoon was luminous and clear. In the three years since his liberation from Hebrew school he had seen Chaya twice, from a distance, coming out of a movie with her parents and her sister, Mara. Now Nathan was suddenly afraid for her, and he was afraid, for the first time ever, of the raucous bodies of his friends.

"Hey, Buster," said Felix E. Scott, leaning forward so that for an instant his thigh lay smooth and cool against Nathan's, "what you going to do to Chaya Feldman?"

"Don't tell me you don't already know, Felix E.," said Buster, heaving the LTD into a small cul-de-sac which Nathan recognized, from some long-ago car pool, as Chaya's street.

"Cut the engine," suggested Tiger Montaine, who excelled in stealthy behavior. He ran his battered little Fiat on siphoned gasoline, filched cigarettes from the supermarket, and had for several months, with Nathan's shocked connivance, been replacing Mrs. Shapiro's codeine pills with extra-strength Tylenol, one at a time. "Don't be waking up that mean Israelite daddy." Chaya's father, Moshe, an oncologist, had been born and raised in Israel, and was, in fact, the most humorless and stern of the one hundred and five fathers Nathan had known in his life. He had a dense black beard and crazy eyebrows, and it was widely half-believed that he kept an Uzi submachine gun, from his days in the army of Israel, hidden under his bed.

Buster turned off the ignition and the car began to glide silently toward Chaya's house. The sudden calm cast a pall over the party and no one spoke; perhaps they were only being careful. Nathan pictured Chaya, asleep, her legs tangled under a light summer blanket; a skeezer! Then, because the ignition had been cut, the steering wheel locked, automatically, and before Buster could do anything they had hopped up over the curb, and came to a stop halfway across somebody's front lawn.

"We're there," said Buster, and everyone laughed. "Now who's going to go knocking on that skeezer's window?"

"I'll go," said Nathan. "I know her."

All of the other boys turned to regard him. Although Nathan felt fairly confident that his friends held him in a certain esteem—his naked presence among them was testimony to that—he had never distinguished himself for his daring, and in fact generally had to be persuaded even to perform minor feats such as dancing with Twanda Woods, or wearing his sneakers without any laces, an affectation which drove his mother out of her mind. And all of the boys knew, for Nathan had been unable, despite himself, to conceal it, that he had never made love to a girl. Emboldened by the malt liquor, he reached out and pushed Felix E. and Tiger in their faces, so that they fell backward into each other.

"I went to Hebrew school with her," he explained.

Perhaps it was only their shock at this uncharacteristic display of fearlessness, but as Nathan stepped out of the car, he noticed a strange look in the eyes of his friends. It was a kind of blank, blinking puzzlement, as though the game had gone awry. Nathan wondered if the whole thing was a lie, if Chaya was not a skeezer at all, and the boys were all of them virgins, and none of them knew what fate awaited him as he began to make his way, naked, barefoot as a child, across the soft grass. He glanced toward the car, toward the three shadowy heads now drawn together in what looked like anxious parley, and almost turned back.

The next moment, however, he felt an entirely new kind of drunkenness; the air was warm against his skin, his lips, his forearms, and—incredibly—moonlight fell upon his penis. He wished that it were a mile to Chaya's house, and not a few short steps, so that he might walk this way a little longer, like a fairy on a moonlit heath. Just this summer—just this month—his body had begun to grow lean, and he strode across the grass with the jangling gait of a young man, delighting in the purpose of his legs. He came to the Feldmans' driveway and zigzagged quickly around to the left side of the house, where he was confronted with a gated, wooden fence. He stopped and contemplated the latticed gate. His breath came quickly now and there was sweat in his eyebrows; a drop spattered against his cheek. Just when he felt the water on his face he saw, through the spaces in the lattice, that a swimming pool, long and unusually narrow, lay beyond. It was not a pool for a pleasure swim; it was a lap pool, no wider than a pair of racing freestylers. Nathan remembered hearing that Dr. Feldman required himself and his family to swim a mile every day.

Pretending for the moment that he was tricksy Tiger Montaine, Nathan held his breath, eased up the steel latch, and slowly let open the gate, without a sound. He walked to the railroad ties that formed the near end of the lap pool and curled his toes over their edge. Thus perched he stood a moment, looking at the reflected moon on the black water and trying to force the tumult in his stomach to abate. He was so nervous that he forgot why he was nervous, and simply hovered at the edge of Chaya's swimming pool, shaking. What was he doing here? Where were his clothes?

He crouched and then slipped, like a deer fleeing a forest fire, into the cool water. He swam across the pool with a light and leisurely stroke. The exercise of his arms and heart in the cold water cleared his thoughts, and left him with a pleasant chlorine sting in his eyes, and when he arrived at the far side of the lap pool, he felt a greater trust in himself and in the general benevolence of a Tuesday night in July. He pulled himself from the pool and tiptoed around to the back of the Feldmans' house. There were some bed-sheets, striped pillowcases, and a pair of bath towels hanging from a revolving clothesline in the backyard, and he considered taking a towel and tying it around his waist. But he felt, obscurely, that there was some advantage in his nakedness, an almost magical advantage that Tiger Montaine, for example, would never have surrendered, and he went over to the windows of the daylight basement in which Chaya had always had her room and stood a moment, with his hands on his wet hips, looking into the dark windows, preparing to wake her. The pool water streamed down his chest to his thighs, raising goosebumps along his legs and arms as Nathan drummed lightly on the glass, attempting a sort of suave seductive rhythm that came out, inexorably, as shave-and-a-hair-cut, two-bits.

⁕ ⁕ ⁕

A light snapped on inside. Someone sat up in the bed—
in Chaya's bed—and this someone did not appear to be
Chaya. She was too tall, and her hair was fuller and darker,
and through the armhole of her sheer short nightgown he
saw the startling contour of a woman's heavy breast. He
turned and began to hightail it out of the backyard, but
the door opened almost immediately, and he turned sheep-
ishly back.

"Is, uh, Chaya here?" he said, in a tone which he hoped
would make him sound too stupid to be doing something
illicit.

"Nathan? Nathan Shapiro?"

"Chaya?"

"What are you doing here? Where are your clothes?"

The light spilling out around her reduced her to a sil-
houette and he could not tell if she looked angry or merely
puzzled. Her voice was a cracked whisper and sounded rather
plaintive in the dark, as though she were also afraid of
getting into some kind of trouble.

"I swam in your pool," Nathan offered, uncertain if this
would explain everything adequately.

"Well, you'd better get out of here. My dad is sleeping
and he hasn't been well."

"Okay," said Nathan. "Good-bye. You got so big,
Chaya." He was staring.

"Puberty," she said. "Ever hear of it?" She stepped back
into the light of her room and smiled a sort of frowny smile
she had always had, and then Nathan felt that he recognized her.

"Chaya, I feel so weird," he said. At the sight of her familiar, serious face he was all at once on the verge of tears.

"Well. Okay, come inside. You have to be quiet."

"Okay."

Nathan followed Chaya into her room, which had the drop ceiling and damp-carpet odor of a basement. On one paneled wall there was a print of *The Starry Night* and an El Al poster with a picture of the Old City of Jerusalem; on the other wall was a painting that Chaya herself must have made, a picture of a palm tree full of bright parrots under a double sun, and Nathan remembered the day he had spent on the Planet Jadis. Beside the painting was an old mounted deer's head, with a split ear, wearing sunglasses and a purple beret. On the table beside her bed was a squat jug lamp with a green shade, a package of Kool cigarettes, and a book by Erica Jong that Nathan had twice been admonished against reading by his grandfather. The circle of light from the lamp seemed to fall almost entirely on the bed, and Nathan averted his eyes, so intimate was the sight of the exposed white sheets and the deep declivity in the pillow. The imprint of her sleeping head, the whole idea of Chaya asleep, struck him as terribly poignant, and he could not look. He heard the creak of the bedsprings and the rustle of sheets as she climbed back into bed.

"I mean you're not ugly, or anything, Nathan," said Chaya, "but put something on, okay?"

"I'm naked!" said Nathan. He looked down at himself, and knew that he was naked. And he saw, as through Chaya's eyes, that in assuming some of its manly proportions

and features, his penis had also begun to take on a con-
comitant forlorn and humorous aspect, sort of like the Jeep
in Popeye cartoons; and he made an apron of his hands
and forearms. This did nothing to conceal, however, the
whiteness of his thighs, or the soft, sad divot of hair around
his left—but not yet his right—nipple.

"There's a towel on the chair."

"I'd better go," said Nathan. He turned and began to
walk out the door, attempting now to cover his probably
ridiculous-looking rear end.

"It's okay, go ahead, put it on, Nathan," said Chaya.

"They brought me," he said, turning again and crab-
walking over to the chair beside Chaya's desk. "The guys.
Tiger and Buster and Felix E." Hurriedly he wrapped the
towel around his waist and tucked in one end, in the fashion
that his grandmother had always referred to, for some reason, as Turkish. It was a scratchy white towel that had
been stolen, to judge from the illegible Hebrew lettering
that was woven like a pattern into one side, from some
hotel in Israel. The lopsided situation of his chest hair
remained a keen embarrassment, and the towel was so
skimpy that the knot at his hip just barely held.

"Are they out there?"

"Yeah. They sent me in. They said—"

"Your hair is all wet." She folded her hands over her
stomach, on the pleat of the bedclothes, and stared at him.
She seemed all in all only mildly surprised to see Nathan,
as though he were visiting her in a dream. Her face had
grown wider, her cheekbones more pronounced, since the
last time he had seen her, and with her tawny skin and her

thick eyebrows and that big, wild hair Nathan thought she looked beautiful and a little scary. He sat down and hugged himself. His teeth were chattering.

"Okay, now I better go." He stood up again.

"Wait," said Chaya. She patted the sheets and indicated that he sit beside her. He came to sit gingerly at her feet, keeping hold with one hand of the tenuous Turkish knot.

"Nathan Shapiro," she said, shaking her head.

"Chaya Feldman."

"Mrs. Falutnick's class."

"Kvit chewink your gum in fronta da r-radio," said Nathan, repeating a favorite inscrutable admonishment of Mrs. Falutnick's in an accent he had not mimicked for six or seven years. Chaya laughed, but Nathan only snorted once through his nose. It had been so long since the days of Mrs. Falutnick's class! He saw himself sitting in a flecked plastic chair at the back of the droning classroom in the Huxley Interfaith Plexus, defacing with moustaches and monkey's fur the grave photographs of Emma Lazarus and Abraham Cahan in his copy of *Adventures in American Jewry,* furtively folding all ten inches of a stick of grape Big Buddy into his mouth when Mrs. Falutnick turned her enormous back on the class, and at this he was unaccountably saddened, and he sighed, startling Chaya out of her dream.

"I heard your parents got a divorce," she said. She looked down, and her long hair splashed her folded hands.

"Yeah," said Nathan, hugging himself again. The shiver that this word produced in him never lasted more than a second or two.

"Why did they?"

"I don't know," Nathan said.

"You don't?"

He thought about it for a few seconds, then shook his head. "I mean they told me, but I forget what they said."

"It's complicated," Chaya offered, helpfully. "People change."

"I think that was part of it," Nathan said, but he didn't believe that there was really any explanation at all.

"Does your dad still live around here?"

"He moved to Boston."

"That's cool," said Chaya. She lifted the curtain of hair from her face and smiled another crooked smile. "I wish my dad would move to Boston."

Nathan said automatically, "No, you don't." He had hitherto managed to forget about the fearsome doctor and he glanced over his shoulder. In the far corner of the room he noticed three large plastic suitcases and a guitar case, neatly lined up as for an imminent departure.

"Where are you going?" he said, gesturing toward the luggage.

"Jerusalem," said Chaya. "Tomorrow. Today, I guess. Later this morning."

"With your family? Or all alone?"

"All alone."

"Are you ever coming back?"

"Of course I am, you," she said. "My father thinks I've gotten—he just wants me to learn to be an Israeli."

"Oh," said Nathan. He was not certain what this entailed, but he suddenly pictured Chaya operating a crane on the bristling lip of a giant construction site in the desert, lowering a turbine generator or a sheaf of I-beams down into the void, the dust of the Negev blowing around her like a long scarf.

"Did they tell you I put out?" said Chaya. "Those guys?"

"Kind of," said Nathan, taken aback, before it occurred to him that this was admitting he had come here for sex, when in fact he had come—why had he come? "It was more like a dare, I guess," he said. "They sort of more or less dared me to come."

"None of them's ever sat on my bed the way you are," said Chaya.

Nathan wondered for a moment exactly what she meant by this, and then, in the next moment, leaned toward her and kissed her lips. This was done only on an off chance and he did not expect that she would take such forceful hold of his body. Startled, without a clue of what he ought to do next, he put one hand on the nape of her neck, the other at the small of her back, and then he lay very still in her arms. He could feel the bones of her hips pressing against him, like a pair of fists, and his lips and somehow his breathing became entangled in her hair. The laundered smell of her bedclothes was overpowering and sweet.

"Are you a virgin, Nathan?" she said, her mouth very close to his.

He considered his reply much longer than he needed to, trying to phrase it as ambiguously as he could. "In a manner of speaking," he said at last, blushing in self-congratulation at the urbanity of this reply.

Her grip upon him relaxed, and she drew back slowly

and then fell back against her pillow, looking calm again. He had the feeling that she had been hoping for some reply totally other than the one he had given. Then Chaya sighed, in a bored, theatrical way that to Nathan's ears sounded very grown up, and he was afraid, at last, that she really might have become a skeezer, that it really was possible to lose track of someone so completely that they turned into someone else without your knowing about it.

"Can you still draw eyeballs?" he said.

"Eyeballs?" she said, her face blank. "Sure, I can."

"Chaya! Mara!" called Dr. Feldman from somewhere in the house. His voice resounded like an axe-blow. "That's enough!"

They both started, and stared a moment at one another as children or as lovers caught.

"Can I tell you something, Nathan?" she said. "When I get to Israel I'm *not* coming back."

"You have to come back," he said, taking her hand.

"Chaya!" thundered Dr. Feldman from very far away. "Go to sleep."

"I'll write you," said Chaya. "Give me your address."

"Sixty-four twenty-three Les Adieux Circle. Is he going to come down here?"

"No," she said. "He thinks you're my little sister. I'll never remember that address. Let me write it down."

"Oh, that's all right," said Nathan, getting up. "You don't need to write me a letter."

"No, wait. Hold on."

She climbed out of bed again, grinning, and went to a blue wooden desk, under the stairs that led up to the first floor of the house. Nathan watched the play of her night-gown across her little behind as she bent over to open a drawer, and then scrabbled around in it, looking for a pen. She found a sheet of pink stationery and began to scratch across it with a Smurf pencil.

"Chaya, I'd better go," said Nathan. He headed for the door.

"Wait!" said Chaya. She was writing furiously now, in a pointed, ribbony script almost like cursive Hebrew, and he waited, one hand on the knob, for her to finish, and hoped that Dr. Feldman would not call out again. When she put down her pen she took a red, white, and blue airmail envelope from another drawer, folded the slip of pink paper in half, slid it into the envelope, and ran her tongue along the flap. Then she bent over the desk again and, brushing her hair from the face of the envelope, wrote out what Nathan knew even from a distance to be his name and address.

"There, I wrote you a letter from Jerusalem," she said, turning toward him. "Don't read it until tomorrow."

"Okay," said Nathan. "Good-bye." He hugged her awkwardly, afraid that he might get an erection, and then eased open the basement door. "Have fun in Jerusalem."

"But I'm already there," she said, continuing in this teasing and mysterious vein. She put a hand on each of his shoulders and kissed him on the cheek. Nathan took the letter from her, a little uncertainly. Probably it was just a bunch of scribble, or an apology for not wanting to have sex with him.

"I know what you're doing!" said Dr. Feldman, with

that weird Yisraeli accent of his, and Nathan went out naked into the night. He was not quite so drunk anymore, and this time the trip around the house, past the swimming pool, did not seem especially fine or ominous. The dog next door to the Feldmans' caught wind of Nathan and began to rail at him, and he ran the rest of the way, all the while trying to determine if Dr. Feldman and his Uzi were in pursuit. As he was running across the Feldmans' yard and into the neighbors', the white towel finally slipped from his waist and fell away, nearly tripping him; he left it to Chaya to explain how it got there, and went naked the rest of the way.

He came around to his side of the car and hesitated with a hand on the door. They were asleep, all three of them, Felix E. and Tiger slumped in opposite corners of the back-seat, Buster stretched out across the front seat of the car. The radio played very softly and threw green light across Buster's thighs. They were snoring with the lustiness of children, and Nathan felt a surge of pity for them and wished that they might just keep on sleeping. When he got into the car, he knew, his friends would want to know what, or rather how much, Chaya had given him; and when he showed them the letter, they would want to read what she had written. He was afraid that its contents might somehow embarrass him, and now he looked for somewhere to conceal it.

At first he considered retrieving the discarded towel, but he was afraid to go back, and anyway, if he wrapped the letter in the towel it would make a pretty suspicious bundle. Then he looked around at the lawn on which they were parked, to see if it held any place in which he could hide the letter, but there was only the silver expanse of lawn, an entire neighborhood of grass and flat moonlight. Under the front windows of the neighbors' house stood one small row of bushes, and he tried poking the envelope deep into this, but you could see it from a mile away, reflecting the light of the moon like a shard of mirror glass, and he retrieved it and looked around again.

Just when he was about to give up and try to hide the letter somewhere in the Frenches' car itself, under a mat, or even in the glove compartment, he spotted a bird feeder, about twenty feet away, hanging from the low branch of a young maple tree. It was shaped like a small transparent house, with a peaked plastic roof and glass walls, about half-filled with birdseed. Nathan unhooked it from its wire and turned it over, his hands shaking with fear and with the aptness of his plan. He pulled off the plastic base of the bird feeder and laid the letter within, burying it amid the smooth and rattling seeds. When he returned the little house to its hook, the letter was nearly invisible, and he trotted back, with a certain air of coolness, to the big yellow LTD.

His friends clambered upright when Nathan climbed back into the car; they were sober and embarrassed, and slapped Nathan constantly on the side of his head. They demanded to know what had happened to Nathan in Chaya's room, and as they drove slowly home he made up a story, filled with sophisticated orgasms, and accurate anatomical impressions, and some bits of sexual dialog in half-remembered Hebrew. The other boys seemed on the whole to believe him, although they were surprised, and blamed malt liquor and hormonal agitation, when halfway through the tale Nathan suddenly burst into tears—then stopped, and resumed his lying account.

The next night Nathan sneaked out of the house after his mother and Ed had gone to sleep. He rode half an hour on his bicycle, through the darkness, to retrieve the letter from Jerusalem. There was no moon, and black shapes seemed to dart and loom across his path. He pulled up in front of the Feldmans' house and contemplated it for a moment, straddling the hard bar of his bike. There was no sign of the towel he had dropped. He hated it that Chaya was not there in her house anymore, that she could so quickly be gone. He had a great curiosity to read what she had written him, but when he crept across to open up the little bird feeder, past the two long scars in the lawn from the wheels of the LTD, he found there was nothing inside it anymore but birdseed. The hairs on the back of his neck stood on end, and he whirled, half expecting to see Chaya, with the letter in her hand, laughing at him from behind the curtain in the low side window of her bedroom. He looked around on the grass, in the row of low shrubs, in the branches of the maple, but the letter was nowhere to be found, and after a few more minutes of baffled searching he got back on his bicycle and pedaled home. As he lay in bed that night he tried to imagine what she might have set down in her letter, what professions of love, what unhappiness, what nonsense, what shame, what news of the planet of her childhood. Then he fell asleep.

* * *

One Saturday a few weeks afterward, Nathan and his stepfather were in the kitchen, trying to work their way out of an incipient argument about whether or not tuna salad ought to be made with chopped gherkins, the way Ed's grandmother had always made it. The dispute was merely the latest and perhaps the most trivial in what was becoming a disheartening routine for Nathan and Ed, and this particular volley of intransigent politeness had just begun to make Nathan's stomach hurt—without inclining him to capitulate—when Mrs. Shapiro-Knipper entered the kitchen, carrying the Saturday mail.

"Two things," she said, handing Nathan two envelopes, one of them tricolor and heartstopping.

"I'm going to put pickles," said Ed. "You'll see. It's an acquired taste."

This time, though everything Ed liked to eat, from raw oysters to pizza with pineapple and ham, seemed to be an acquired taste, Nathan let it pass. He rose from the kitchen table and carried the two letters out into the hallway and down to his bedroom. The second, in a plain business envelope, was evidently from his father, who had never before sent a letter to Nathan, and Nathan sat on his bed for a long time without opening them, just thinking about mailmen, and sealed envelopes, and the mysteries of the post.

He supposed that the neighbor had found Chaya's letter hidden in the bird feeder before Nathan could retrieve it, and had finally gotten around to affixing a stamp to it and sending it along. Since, in the past weeks, Nathan had decided that he was in love with Chaya, and had been busy erecting all the necessary buttresses and towers and fluttering pennants in his imagination, the surprise arrival of her letter, which he had presumed lost, was a delicious addition to the structure, and he delayed as long as he could stand before finally tearing open the envelope.

DEAR NATHAN,

Sometimes it is very hot here. I have a thousand boyfriends. It is scary if a gun goes off in the night.

You made me laugh a lot of times in class I remember.

"Take it easy."

Love,

CHAYA

He was sharply disappointed. He hated the fact that he had made her laugh, for one; and it angered him, unreasonably, he knew, that all of the other things—and there were so few of them—she had written were hypothetical, as insubstantial as her Planet of the Birds, or as his parents' marriage, or as the baby that was growing in his stepmother's belly. He stuffed the bogus letter back into the envelope and tore it to pieces.

He was still feeling bad when at last he brought himself to open the letter from his father. It was a brief, barely legible note, on a sheet of legal paper. After some facetious chitchat about the Red Sox and Ricky's karate lessons, Nathan's father had written, "Your mother tells me that you have made some new friends and she is a little worried because you're going around with your shoes untied. Tie your shoelaces. Don't be angry with us, Nate. I know that everything seems different now but you have to get used to it. I will always love you as much as I will love any new Shapiros that come along."

"Nathan?" his mother called to him through the door of his room. "Come on and eat."

"I hate it with gherkins," said Nathan, but his heart had gone out of the argument, and he stood up to join his mother and Ed for lunch. Hastily he dried his eyes, and scrambled to gather up the letter from his father and the scraps of Chaya's letter that were scattered across his bed. It was as he laid them carefully in the Roi-Tan cigar box in which he kept his most important papers that he noticed the strange and beautiful postage stamp in the torn corner of the airmail envelope, and the postmark, printed in an alien script.

BOOKS BY MICHAEL CHABON

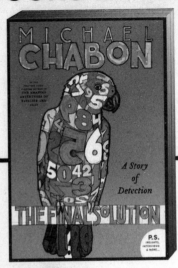

THE FINAL SOLUTION
A Story of Detection

ISBN 0-06-077710-9 (paperback)

Retired to the English
countryside, an eighty-nine-
year old man, rumored to be a
once-famous detective, is more
concerned with his beekeeping
than his fellow man. Into his life
wanders Linus Steinman, nine
years old and mute, who has
escaped from Nazi Germany with
his sole companion: an African
grey parrot.

"Exceptional."
   —*New York Times Book Review*

THE MYSTERIES OF PITTSBURGH
A Novel

ISBN 0-06-079059-8 (paperback)

A funny, tender, coming-of-
age novel.

"Remarkable. . . . What makes
this book—and Chabon—worth
our attention is [that] Chabon
has chosen not merely to record
all the ills of an oversexed,
overindulged generation with
nowhere to go but to bed or to a
bar; he has chosen to explore, to
enter this world and try to find
what makes it work, why love
and friendship choose to visit
some, and deny others."
   —*Los Angeles Times*

Look for *The Yiddish Policeman's Union* coming Winter 2006!